D0591352

Soldier Boys

Soldier Boys

David Richards

Thistledown Press Ltd.

Canadian Cataloguing in Publication Data
Richards, David, 1953 –
Soldier boys
ISBN 1-895449-06-5
I. Riel Rebellion, 1885. Juvenile fiction
I. Title.
PS858.I34S64 1993 jC813'.54   C93-098032-8
PZ7.R53So 1993

Cover painting by Armand Paquette with permission from the
Batoche National Historic Site
Book design by A.M. Forrie
Typeset by Thistledown Press
Printed and bound in Canada by AGMV Marquis

Thistledown Press Ltd.
633 Main Street
Saskatoon, Saskatchewan
S7H 0J8

Thistledown Press gratefully acknowledges the financial assistance of
the Canada Council for the Arts, the Saskatchewan Arts Board, and
the Government of Canada through the Book Publishing Industry
Development Program for its publishing program.

To Stella, James and Louise

I would like to acknowledge the editorial work of Seán Virgo. His insight not only regarding the characters and the story, but also the author, was greatly appreciated. Lynda Newson deserves special recognition for her support and guidance. I would also like to thank the Cree Community for their generous editorial advice.

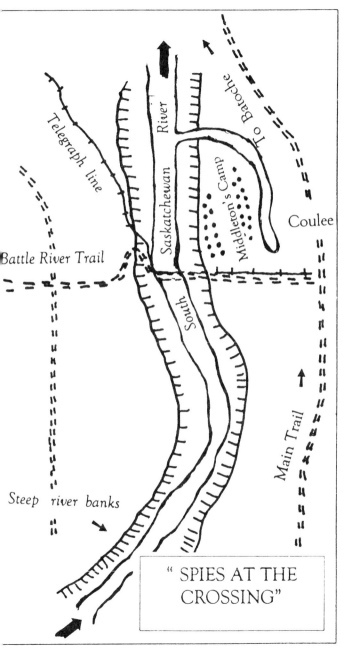

Telegraph line

Saskatchewan River

To Batoche

Middleton's Camp

Coulee

Battle River Trail

South

Main Trail

Steep river banks

" SPIES AT THE
CROSSING"

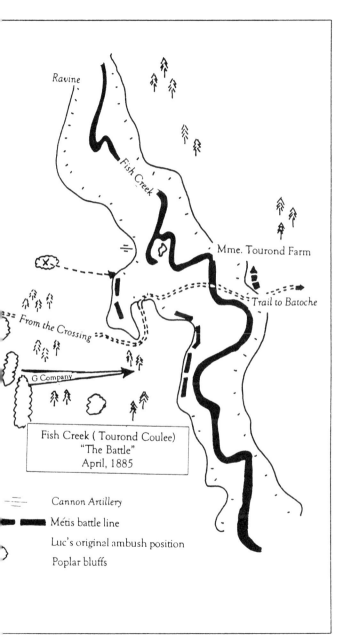

Ravine

Fish Creek

Mme. Tourond Farm

Trail to Batoche

From the Crossing

G Company

Fish Creek (Tourond Coulee)
"The Battle"
April, 1885

Cannon Artillery

Métis battle line

Luc's original ambush position

Poplar bluffs

CONTENTS

1.   Unrest

W ho's the next applicant?" snapped a voice from within the small office.

The soldier consulted his list. "Thomas C. Kerslake, sir."

"Well send him in and be quick about it!" The voice was deep, full of authority.

Tom tugged on the cuffs of his coat, tightened his tie, and walked into the office. Remembering his uncle's coaching, he stopped three paces in front of the desk, put his heels together, and stared straight ahead. The man sitting behind the desk said nothing; he eyed Tom critically. The silence was unending. Was there something wrong? Tom remembered his Uncle's last piece of advice, "Don't slouch boy; stand straight. Soldiers don't slouch." Tom tried to stretch a bit taller.

The man rose slowly, leaned forward and looked directly into Tom's eyes. Tom tried desperately not to fidget and returned the stare as evenly as he could. The commander of G Company of the Winnipeg Rifles wore a huge walrus moustache with the tips waxed and curled into little half circles that almost touched his equally large sideburn whiskers. Other than that he had scarcely a hair on his head. The sight of the shining bald dome sur-rounded by bushy whiskers looked so odd that Tom had to bite down on his tongue to keep from laughing. If he suddenly laughed in Captain Lashbrooke's face, he would stand no chance of getting the job.

"Thomas C. Kerslake," the Captain said again, quietly. "How old are you, boy?"

"I'm thirteen sir."

"You know, of course, that the minimum age for buglers is fourteen?"

Tom nodded.

"Then please tell me, young sir, why I should take you on when you are only thirteen years old?"

Tom was ready with his reply.

"Actually I'll be fourteen this April, sir; that's only two months away, and I play the trumpet in the church band, and I'm already familiar with several of the regiment's bugle calls. Also I'll be available to go to the summer training camp this year, and . . . ."

Captain Lashbrooke raised his hand to cut Tom short. "Yes, yes quite so, but we are not the church band, boy. The Winnipeg Rifles are a regiment of the Queen's army. We are soldiers. I can train a monkey to play the bugle. What I need is a good soldier who can work at my side in battle and function as a company bugler!"

His voice rose in volume and power. He tucked one hand into the front of his coat and raised the other hand up as though pointing to heaven. "You may be able to play some tunes in the church hall but will you be any good to me when the bullets are flying and the enemy is hard upon us? I have a vision of battle in which the men of Winnipeg will earn everlasting glory. Do you have the mettle to stand with such men?"

Tom stayed rigidly at attention. Was he supposed to say something?

The Captain was a militiaman who came to the armouries a couple of times a month for training. In reality he was a lawyer. He must have learned to speak dramatically from all the time he spent in court. Tom felt so intimidated by the imposing figure that he decided to say nothing.

Captain Lashbrooke came out from behind the desk and circled around Tom, like a hawk above a gopher. Finally he seemed to make a decision.

"I don't know what I'm supposed to do with a skinny thirteen year old boy, but at least you're not very tall. That will do, Kerslake; you may leave."

Tom flushed; was that it? He had expected that Captain Lashbrooke would want to hear him play the bugle, or ask him questions about soldiering, or do something other than just call him skinny and short. He turned and left the office, stung by the comments. He really was skinny and he *was* just a trumpet player for the church band. The suit he had pressed for the interview was too old and didn't fit very well. He tugged at the cuffs again to make them stay down over his wrists.

It was all clear now. He hadn't really stood a chance to get the bugler job, the other two boys applying were much bigger and stronger, and he knew one of them was fourteen already. He had really gotten his hopes up, especially when his uncle had urged him to apply for the position, but now it had turned out to be a big joke. The more he thought about it the more embarrassed and angry he became. He didn't have to stand for insults about his looks, or his courage. He *could* be a good soldier, and anyway, Lashbrooke wasn't very tall himself, and he was bald. Who needed to be bugler for such a man?

He trudged home through the snow-covered streets, hardly noticing the cold February wind whipping his face. The Captain's cruel words kept running through his head. He could now think of all sorts of clever things he should have said instead of just meekly leaving the office. He even considered going back to give the man a piece of his mind but that wasn't realistic. Thirteen year old boys do not answer back to important lawyers.

He was in a thoroughly foul mood when he reached home. He hurried through the back yard to the porch and slammed the door as he passed into the kitchen. The stove's warmth chased the frost from his face. Supper was cooking and it smelled delicious, but it held little comfort for him today.

He crossed the empty kitchen, and climbed the stairs to his bedroom. The stove pipe from the kitchen came up through the floor, turned a sharp right angle and attached to the chimney which protruded from one wall. The stove was going full blast and the heat from the pipe made his small room quite cozy and warm. Tom threw off his parka, hat and mitts, then jumped onto his bed where he sat cross-legged looking out the dormer window onto the street. He hadn't been there long when his depression was interrupted by a high pitched screech from the kitchen below.

"MY FLOOR! WHO did this to my floor?"

It was his older sister, Violet. He should have swept the snow and bits of horse manure from his boots when he came in. He could picture the dirty puddles of water tracking across her kitchen floor which she always seemed to have "just cleaned." Now she would give him a scolding as though he was some irresponsible child and she was the lady of the house. Well she could think again. One humiliation was enough for the day and he wouldn't take any of her nonsense. She yelled again but he continued to stare out the window. Then he heard her footsteps thumping up the stairs, followed seconds later by a loud hammering on his door.

"Tom, are you in there?"

"Yes, and you can stay out." His voice was belligerent.

The door swung open and banged against the back wall. Violet, her face angry and red, marched in. Where Tom was short, Violet was tall. While Tom was often shy and nervous, Violet was self-confident and strong. Even in her coarse work blouse and heavy skirt she was attractive. At least young men were always showing up at the house with some excuse, often pretending to have business with Father. She never had much to do with them, but that didn't stop them from coming back. As she was fond of telling anyone who would listen, she was destined for better things than any local boy could offer. Right now, she was destined to make *his* life difficult.

"Don't speak to me like that, you young pup! You made a mess of my kitchen and I've JUST CLEANED THE FLOOR."

Tom stared out at the street below. He knew he couldn't beat her in an argument so he just ignored her, which would really drive her crazy.

"You can take yourself downstairs right now and clean up those tracks," she continued, poking him in the chest with her finger.

Tom still said nothing.

"So it's the silent treatment, is it? We'll see what Father says about this, Mister!" She stomped out, slamming the door.

Moments later Tom heard his father come in the front door and immediately afterwards the muffled voice of his sister. When his father eventually appeared at the top of the stairs, Tom opened the bedroom door without being asked. The weary look on Father's face dissolved Tom's anger. Father put in long hard days at work, he didn't need to come home to a squabble in his own house. Tom appreciated this, but sometimes he couldn't help arguing with Vi. It just happened.

"Thomas, I will not have you fighting with Violet. You know full well that she is the woman of this house. She works hard and takes on a great responsibility for a seventeen year old girl. You must show her respect, do you understand?"

Tom felt he had hit rock bottom. Captain Lashbrooke had obviously been able to see how childish he really was. It was little wonder he had been turned down as the Company bugler. He glanced out the window to avoid his father's eyes and saw a tall figure wrapped in a greatcoat and topped with a fur hat coming in the back yard. His father followed his gaze.

"All right, your Uncle Jim is here. Let's go meet him and say nothing more of this incident."

Tom liked his Uncle Jim as much as he liked anyone. Jim always had a new story, or a new idea, or something exciting on the go. Just his enthusiasm for life was infectious and seeing him arrive for supper brightened Tom up a bit. Down in the kitchen the dirty puddles still marked the floor and Violet took great care to step over them as she bustled around the kitchen making the final preparations for supper.

"All finished pouting?" she snapped. "Then maybe you can get the mop and. . . ."

The door from the back porch burst open and Uncle Jim swept into the room.

"VI! How's the prettiest little homemaker in Winnipeg?" He tossed his fur hat on the table. His heavy boots clumped loudly as he crossed the kitchen, catching Violet around the waist to give her a hug. Uncle Jim hadn't knocked the snow and mud from his boots; they left an even worse mess on the floor. Violet blushed at the hug and looking down at the wet tracks yelped:

"Uncle James! Look at the floor, and I've just washed it!"

This time her voice wasn't a high-pitched shriek. She wore a huge smile. Jim pretended to hang his head in shame and cringed as though she would hit him. Then he did a quick tap dance over to Father, and punched him playfully in the ribs. Last he looked at Tom and became very serious. Normally Jim had a joke for Tom but today for some reason he looked positively stern.

"George, I suppose you haven't heard what this son of yours has been up to at the armoury today, have you?"

Tom shrank back a step. Surely his Uncle would be on his side?

"As a matter of fact, Thomas and I were discussing something quite different. He hasn't mentioned the bugler business," replied Father.

Uncle Jim unbuttoned his greatcoat and it fell open to reveal the dark green uniform of the Winnipeg Rifles. Uncle Jim was the Colour Sergeant in G Company. It was he who had suggested that Tom apply for the bugler position. Jim had been down at the armouries drilling some of the new recruits today and he had no doubt heard all about the interview.

"I shouldn't wonder he never mentioned his performance today," Jim continued, "quite a disgrace for the Kerslake family."

Now even the prospect of a supper with Uncle Jim had turned sour. And then Jim reached slowly into the deep skirt pocket of the great coat and drew out a bugle. A sparkling brass bugle, complete with a blood-red lanyard and green tassels. It was beautiful. Tom did not understand.

"This boy here wins the position of Bugler for G Company, the 90th Battalion Winnipeg Rifles, and then leaves for home without taking the darn thing! Can you understand such forgetfulness?" Jim now had a broad smile on his face, and he marched forward to shake Tom's hand and present him with the horn.

"I took a few minutes to shine her up, but from now on you take good care of it, lad. It's regimental stores and I've signed for it."

Tom was stunned. How could this be? Had Uncle Jim pulled some strings or caused trouble on his behalf?

"But Captain Lashbrooke said I was skinny, short, and underage. Did you change his mind?"

He handed the bugle back to his uncle.

"I can't accept the position if I didn't win it fair and square."

Big Jim let out a laugh, and pushed the horn away.

"You just don't know that windbag like I do, Tom. I didn't have to say anything. Lashbrooke sought me out at the end of drill today and told me he had chosen you."

Jim stuck one hand into the front of his tunic and looked down his nose. He croaked deeply, imitating the Captain's voice.

"Your skill on the instrument and smart bearing will be an asset to the company!" He snorted and slapped Tom on the back.

"In truth he's the most conceited, vain man I have ever met. He wanted to ensure that his bugler wouldn't overshadow him. He *wants* a short bugler! He's no fool," laughed Jim. "He got the best man for the job and he can look good to boot."

Tom was giddy with relief. He put the bugle down, darted out to the porch closet for the mop, and cleaned up both sets of footprints. Vi actually beamed at him.

The supper was one of great delight to Tom. His status in the family seemed to have been elevated from that of the baby to more of an adult. Yet he noticed that whenever the conversation turned towards his service as a bugler, Father seemed to be quiet and concerned. Tom proudly told them about Captain Lashbrooke's vision of the Winnipeg Rifles gaining glory in battle.

"Glory? He has obviously obtained a different view of war than I have. Perhaps because he's never been in one." Father scowled. He stabbed his fork into a potato and waved it at Tom.

"Don't believe everything you hear, my boy. Especially in the Army!"

Both his father and uncle had fought for the Union army in the great Civil War in the United States twenty years earlier. His father had been twenty and Uncle Jim only eighteen. It was hard to picture them as such young men. They told funny stories about army life and sometimes they talked about the hardships. They never spoke about the actual fighting.

"But what about the picture on the mantle?" Tom protested. He left the table to retrieve it. It showed his father and Jim standing side by side, in their uniforms. Carved into the wood picture frame were the words, "23rd Wisconsin Infantry – Glorious Shilo."

He ran his finger over the inscription. "You fought like heros at the Battle of Shilo. What's so wrong with the Winnipeg Rifles winning a glorious victory?"

"We were good soldiers, Tom. We fought for what we thought was right," explained Uncle Jim. "But your father means there's not much glamour to be seen on the actual battlefield."

"But Captain Lashbrooke says battle is good for you, it tests a man's mettle."

"The more I hear about Lashbrooke, the less I like him. I was never too keen on Tom joining the Rifles anyway, and now he's putting these ideas in the boy's head." Tom's father shook his head. "One of the reasons you and I came to Canada was to get away from that kind of stupidity."

"I know, I know," soothed Jim. "But there's a big difference between Canada and the States. The militia is just a bunch of Saturday soldiers." Jim shrugged. "There's no war. Blowhards like Lashbrooke can use the militia to give themselves commissioned rank and a title. Come on George, think. If there was real trouble the British regulars would do all the fighting."

Tom's father was unconvinced.

"What would your mother say if she were alive, eh Tom? Jim's a bachelor, he can run off to the army if he wants, but I want you, me and Vi to be together as a family."

Tom stayed quiet. He well knew his father's views on their family. Father, Mother and Vi — as a baby — had gone with Jim to homestead in Minnesota after the Civil War. But there had been constant fighting between the Sioux Indians and the United States Army, so they had come up to Canada. Tom was born a Canadian, but he never knew his mother for she had died when he was born. Father and Jim, then later Vi had raised him. They had built a happy home in Winnipeg over the last fourteen years.

"Well, I'd quit the militia in a minute if you'd go west with me this spring." Jim was off on his new pet project. "The railway's opened up thousands of miles of new land." He threw his arms out wide. "We could make our fortunes, us four."

"Winnipeg is alright, but I'm not so sure about farther west, Jim," Father countered. "I'm doing well with the Company now and I'm up for promotion to assistant manager. I can get Thomas apprenticed to the Bay in little more than a year, and your freighting business is successful. Why would anyone want to move out into the wilds?"

"Aye, now there's where you're wrong, my older brother," said Jim lightly, fumbling in his pocket for his tobacco pouch. "Out in the Saskatchewan country they're giving land away. If we get there first we could own half the territory. It would see our fortunes made!"

Tom and Vi quietly moved away from the table and began clearing up while the men lit their pipes and got deep into the discussion.

Tom said it to himself, "Saskatchewan Territory." Even the name was exciting. What a dream — taming a wilderness, making his fortune alongside Father and Jim. Maybe not much of a life for Vi, her dreams seemed to be stuck in Montreal or Toronto. The thought of Vi going down east to a college was scary. Would she really leave them if she got the chance?

"Tom, quit daydreaming and move those dishes!" She bustled past him carrying a basin of hot water. "And don't spill anything on my floor."

Well, bossy or not, he'd still miss her. He dumped a load of dirty dishes into the basin, and soapy water splashed over the side.

"Tom! I just said be careful."

He sighed. Land baron on the Saskatchewan? More likely a bookkeeper in the Hudson Bay Company office.

Bedtime came, but he couldn't sleep. He watched as the frost formed its icy patterns on the window, and listened to the men downstairs still arguing about going west. The bugle hung by its lanyard from a hook on the wall. The moonlight that filtered through the frosted window glinted off the curving brass bell of the horn. West or not, at last he was a member of the regiment with a job as important as any man, and that was enough for now.

* * *

"And I have been lazy over my lessons, Father. I don't like books or reading and especially not English, so I didn't study as hard as I said I would."

Luc twisted his mitts nervously. He shifted slightly on the rough plank bench and tugged the bulky hem of his Hudson Bay Blanket parka. The priest's shadow was outlined on the threadbare cotton sheet that hung as a divider between them. Luc's mother prayed softly, her voice seeped through the blanket that formed the wall. What could she have to confess? Luc smiled, his Mother was a better Catholic than the priests.

"Aaahum! Continue?"

"Oh! Uh, that's everything, Father" Luc fidgeted again and glanced at the shadow.

"Then your sins are forgiven you, in the name of the Father, the Son and the Holy Ghost." The priest's outstretched hand dropped down then moved left and right in the sign of the cross. Luc lightly touched his own forehead, breast, and shoulders.

"For your penance, say five Hail Mary's and one Our Father."

Luc rose, pushed through the blanket and walked quietly past his Mother toward the front of the church.

"Luc Goyette!"

Luc whirled around and a stocky figure clad in a long black robe stepped from the other side of the confessional. Father Fourmond's square face crinkled into a grin. He scratched his fringe of close cropped white hair and pointed at Luc's Mother.

"I could be busy for quite a long time," he whispered. "So I may not get a chance to see you before Mass. I wanted to tell you that your last essay was good. Very good indeed." He chuckled softly. "And don't worry. I'll never ask for one in English!"

"Thank you for that Father." The priest ducked back into the confessional as Luc's Mother rose to enter. Luc made his way to the bench occupied by his Father and

the two little children. Kneeling, he crossed himself,
muttered five Hail Mary's, crossed again, then sat up on
the bench. A moment later he remembered the Our
Father so he knelt and said it rapidly.

A steady stream of people flowed into the church to
line up in front of the three confessionals. Luc could not
concentrate on a prayer or even a single religious thought.
A daydream carried him out of the church and south
toward the river bend near their farm. A thick stand of
poplars sheltered his trapline there. There would be no
chance to check it today, but he would go early tomorrow.

Gradually the confessionals emptied and Mass
began. Luc went through the service mechanically.
Whoever heard of a nine day Novena? Father Fourmond
droned on into the sermon. *Bichon.* That was the colour
of the horse he would buy this spring. Bichon with a
white star on the forehead.

"As Jesus said to his flock, I say to you my children:
Blessed are the Meek, for they shall. . . ."

And fast. It might not be big, or powerful, but his
pony would have speed and endurance. Heavy horses
were for farming; light horses were for hunting and
racing.

"Those among us who presume to defy the law of
the land are NOT MEEK. Pride and vanity will lead to
their downfall. . . ."

What would prices for fur be at Carlton this spring?
Even if they were as good as last year he would get enough
for his horse. Luc strained his neck to peer over the

congregation. Napoleon Nault sat five rows back. The Naults had the best horses between Prince Albert and Duck Lake.

"As a priest I am duty bound. I can *not* extend sacraments to anyone who takes up arms in defiance of the police. It is against God's Law and. . . ."

Prices last spring were low. Luc stuck a finger inside his moccasin to scratch thoughtfully. If they went up then he would have enough money to buy from the Nault family. Maybe even enough for a rifle as well?

"Gentle Jesus, Meek and Mild! Did our Saviour take up the sword to fight Pontius Pilate? NO! Then who are we, my brothers and sisters, to rise up in arms? Surely we must take our lead from the Prince of Peace who. . . ."

The old shotgun was alright. But a rifle, even a plains percussion rifle would be so much better. A repeater was out of the question of course — too expensive. But a forty-five calibre rifle would be perfect. He squinted, aiming along the side of the altar to line up an imaginary deer. He could use his father's bullet mold, and powder was cheaper than brass cartridges.

"ARRÊTE! MON DIEU ARRÊTE!"

Luc jumped six inches straight up, blushing with guilt. Father Fourmond stood rigid at the pulpit, his face white except for a bright red dot on each cheek. The priest glowered furiously at the back of the church. Luc's head swivelled.

Louis Riel stood in the centre aisle, one clenched fist raised above his head. The other hand clutched a huge bible. Black unruly curls sprouted from beneath a wool tuque to nestle against the heavy collar of his coat. His lips were drawn back thin, in a snarl. Riel's gaze flickered over the crowd and locked onto Luc's eyes. It was like the last shaft of light at sunset, beaming over the horizon to blind him for an instant, then it was gone.

Riel's fist pounded onto the bible.

"You are NOT GOD! The sacraments are God's gift. They do not belong to Vital Fourmond!"

He stalked up the aisle to face the priest.

"Moses defied the Egyptians. David slew the Philistines. The Métis people will defy the Canadians and we will slay the police."

He turned to face the congregation and held the bible outstretched in both hands.

"I have a prophesy. God has called me as a prophet for the Métis nation and HE will not be denied."

Riel strode down the aisle and out of the church. Gabriel, Edouard, Isidore and Eli Dumont followed him. Several others rose hesitantly, then rushed out the door after the Dumonts. An invisible hand seemed to pull Luc to his feet, urging him to follow Riel. One of the Carrieres pushed past him to leave but Luc stood rooted. He looked down at the beaded pattern on his moccasins.

"Api!" his Mother's whisper broke the spell and he sat heavily.

A draft of winter air swirled around him as Carriere slammed the door. The cold settled on him and he shivered. What were Riel and the Dumonts going to do? Father Fourmond hurried through the rest of mass and disapeared into the vestry.

The air outside the church felt good. Luc sucked in a huge lungful and blew a billow of frosty breath. Most of the people were milling around in the space between the Church and the Rectory to shelter from the freezing wind.

"Adrien! Here, over here!"

Luc's father shouldered through the crowd toward a man wearing a bright blue capote (sporting a red *ceinture noue*). Louis Marion. Luc's stomach gripped with fear. Marion was one of Gabriel Dumont's oldest companions, and a wild-man by reputation. Luc took Marguerite and Jerome by the hand and followed his parents.

"Well Goyette, are you with the Priests or Riel?"

Adrien faced Marion squarley and stared him in the eye. Luc held his breath.

"The priests of course."

Marion barked a short laugh. "Ho! You've got guts, Adrien Goyette. Always knew that, I guess." He scratched his stubble beard and squinted at Luc.

"And you? I thought you were going to walk right out in the middle of mass! Are you with the Dumonts?"

"How dare you, Louis Marion! Leave him alone. He's a boy — only fourteen. Don't drag him into this."

Luc's face flushed with embarrassment, but he really was glad his mother had answered for him. The truth was, he didn't know himself which side he would choose.

Marion laughed again, but kindly. "How right you, are Madame Goyette. I wish none of us had to pick sides. Me? " He shrugged. "I'm for the priests also."

"But you're Gabriel's oldest friend!" Adrien exclaimed. "You've been with him since the battle of Grand Coteau in '57!"

"Ha! You're right, Adrien." He stared at Luc. "And I was only fifteen years old in that fight."

Luc blushed again.

"Yet you'll oppose him now" Adrien continued. "Why?"

Marion pawed his foot in the snow like a buffalo scratching for grass, and looked sideways. "What did you think of Riel's performance just now?"

"Awas!" Luc's mother spat the word. "He will go to hell if he acts like that in God's house! He interrupted the divine service; he didn't take his hat off; and he didn't even genuflect or cross himself when he stood right before the altar! And did you hear him? He called Père Fourmond by his first name!"

Louis nodded slowly. "Yes, all that. And he calls himself a prophet, God's messenger. Do you believe it?"

"No of course not." Adrien shook his head. "But I think *he* believes it and so does Gabriel Dumont."

"Prophet!" Mother put her hand on Luc's shoulder. "Luc knows better than that! Do prophets wear tuques and capotes?"

Images of Moses and John the Baptist flashed in Luc's mind. He'd seen his Mother pore over those pictures in the bible a hundred times.

"No, the prophets all wear robes and God's light shines on them."

His mother beamed triumphant. "Louis Riel isn't even a *Medicine Man.* Much less a priest or a prophet."

Luc suppressed a smirk. His mother, half Cree, often mixed Indian spirits into the Catholic church.

"I agree, Madame Goyette." Marion glanced over his shoulder towards the knot of people clustered around Riel and Gabriel Dumont. "I think he's crazy and I'll have nothing to do with him. Still he's powerful and he has the Dumonts that could be dangerous."

"Will you leave Batoche then?" Adrien asked.

"Leave? Mon dieu No!" He laughed out loud. "The Dumonts don't frighten Louis Marion!" He thumped his fist against his chest. "The danger is what makes it all worthwhile! Just like the old days except instead of challenging the Blackfoot I challenge the Dumonts and *Uneeyen.*"

Laughing to himself, Marion moved off through the crowd. His parents fell into conversation with the Parenteaus, so Luc went on ahead with the little children.

Jerome and Marguerite pelted him with snowballs then ran squealing down the trail past the Rectory. Luc chased them, growling and snarling, pretending to be a bear.

"Ha, Ha, Big Bear. You can't catch me!" shrieked Marguerite.

Her stubby legs flailed through the snow at the edge of the trail. Luc roared and lumbered after her. They soon reached the horse and cutter, sheltered in a heavy poplar bluff on the crest of the ridge that overlooked Batoche.

Far below, the houses and shops clustered near the crossing where the frozen expanse of the river turned sharply to the north. Luc could clearly see Letendre's two-story general store on Main Street. Surrounding the village, the narrow Métis fields ran back from the river's edge in long, snow-covered stripes.

A snowball smacked him hard on the side of his head, he stumbled backward into a snowdrift and fell. A handsome dark face framed by two long braids peered from behind the cutter.

"*Waniska, N'Sjayasis!*"

"It's Pierre!" squealed Jerome. He and Marguerite launched themselves like two baby wolverines and tackled the young man, wrestling with him in the snow. Marguerite, holding tightly to one braid, sat on his chest pinning him. Jerome waddled up with an armful of snow and dumped it squarely on Pierre's face.

"*Ekaya! Ekayawiya* Save me, *N'Sjayasis*."

Luc, once more the growling bear, crawled towards them and swatted the two children. "It's Big Bear! Run

Jerome, Run!" They climbed giggling to the highest seat
on the cutter while Luc helped Pierre to his feet and
dusted the snow from his face.

"Pierre, it's so good to see you again."

"And you, *Mistahyamaskwa*."

Luc was puzzled a moment, *Mistahyamaskwa*? Then
he laughed, Big Bear, of course!

"Hey, don't tell me you're forgetting your Cree. Is
your father still forcing English down your throat?"

"OOh yes," Luc groaned. "Please don't remind me.
I've already confessed my English sins once today."

"The only sin is learning it in the first place. Between
the priests, the rectory school and the English, you'll end
up just like Jean if you don't watch out."

Luc merely grunted and turned away. Pierre couldn't
understand; *he* was free to come and go as he pleased.

"I'm sorry *N'Sjayasis*. I meant no harm. Jean was my
best friend. Look, I got back from One Arrow's reserve
yesterday and found this at the post office." He pulled a
slightly crumpled envelope from inside his tunic. "It's
from Jean, I knew you'd be at church today so I brought
it for you."

Luc's temper evaporated — a letter from Jean! He
never could stay angry with Pierre.

"Then you must come home with us for dinner and
hear what it says. Help me hitch up the cutter, my parents
will be along in a moment."

The Goyette cutter hissed over the snow-packed trail
heading south of Batoche. Pierre trotted behind them on

his pony. The little children teased Luc, using their new word.

"Bad *Mistahyamaskwa* — Bad old big bear," they chanted.

Three miles south of Batoche, Adrien guided the cutter off the main trail and turned right on a smaller path toward the South Saskatchewan River. A half mile farther on they entered a shallow ravine that dropped gradually down to the river. The ravine was filled to the brim with a tangle of grey leafless poplar. The bush was cut back in a neat open rectangle and snuggled cozy in the centre of the clearing lay the Goyette farm.

The tall house made of large squared logs, plastered with clay and whitewashed clean as the new snow, stood on the highest side of the clearing. From it the two sheds, the granary and the white hump of the root cellar marched downhill to the barn and corral at the bottom. Luc and Pierre got the horses into the barn before making their way to the house.

Luc's mother had just built up the fire in the stove. The warmth touched his cold cheeks when he came through the door. The first floor of the house was one open room with the stove and kitchen tables taking up most of it. The far end contained two large chairs which stood on either side of a small lamp table. Pierre and Adrien drifted into the two chairs; the children disappeared upstairs. While his mother prepared the meal Luc busied himself hauling water and fetching wood. Jean's unopened letter was laid carefully in the centre of the table.

Soon they all sat facing steaming plates full of boiled potatoes, turnips, fish, and venison. Mother nodded; everyone made the sign of the cross and bowed their heads.

"Bless this food which we are about to receive through thy bounty, Christ our lord, Amen."

Luc was famished and attacked his food. The venison was a special treat and he was careful to soak up all the drippings with a *galette*.

"I'll have to stop calling you *N'Sjayasis* if you keep eating like that!" Pierre grinned and winked at Adrien. "He won't be my *little* brother for long."

Luc just grunted and kept on chewing.

"Pierre?" Jerome's voice chirped.

"Oui, Monsieur Jerome."

"Why do you call Luc your little brother? He's *my* brother, not yours."

"But that's the beauty of the Cree tongue Jerome. One word can mean many things. *N'Sjayasis* means I love Luc as though he was my little brother."

"Oh." Jerome returned to his food.

"Well, I daresay Luc appreciates the Cree tongue more than the English, judging by the progress he's making," said Father.

"But I can *speak* English — it's the reading and the writing that are tough," Luc protested. "Anyway, most of the boys I know can't even read French, much less English. It's not fair. . . ."

"You won't get far at the college with that attitude. . . ."

"Stop it you two!" Mother interupted. "Pierre didn't come here to listen to an argument. How is your Mother, Pierre, is she happy back on the reserve?"

"Very happy." Pierre stuffed a *galette* loaded with mashed turnips into his mouth and chewed loudly. "She still misses Pere but I think she is better back with all her relatives. Everyone in Batoche was kind, but she needed some family after he died. Between freighting and hunting I'm not home much. I'm eighteen now and must earn my keep."

Mother reached out to take Pierre's hand in her own. "I pray for her and you. I know she is full blood and not raised Christian, but your father was Catholic and you were baptised. Don't you think you should make an effort to come back to the church?"

Pierre fidgeted in his seat and glanced to Luc for help.

"Oh Maman! Not everybody is the same as us. Me, I'd much rather travel and hunt than become a priest."

"That's enough, Luc." Father's voice was tipped with warning.

"You may read the letter now if we're all finished eating."

The two men lit their pipes and leaned back on their chairs. Luc opened the envelope and read out loud. It was similar to Jean's other letters. He told them how much he missed them, and all about his studies. The mathematics and science subjects were hard but the literature and languages were going extremely well. He might be accepted to study law, or even to prepare for the priesthood, which was his mother's great wish.

When Luc finished, his mother carefully packed the letter away with all of Jean's other letters in a small tin box. She snuffled and wiped one eye.

"Madame Goyette, why do you take such care with Jean's old mail?" Pierre touched the tin box. "I think that you, like me, cannot read, so why do you collect them?"

"Only a man would ask such a question, never a mother," she answered with just a touch of rebuke in her voice. "These letters were written by my son's hand; they are his thoughts held out to me so that I can touch them. They *are* my son Jean; they are the only way I can be with him. This box is my talisman." She shook the tin. "Of course I also pray for him every night, and the protection of our Saviour is the strongest medicine of all."

"Of course, Madame Goyette, I should have known better," Pierre said hastily. He knew that if Mother got started on religion it could turn into a long sermon.

"I suppose you'll be off to Montreal yourself in less than two years Luc?" Pierre changed the subject. "Will the legacy cover Luc's education, Adrien?"

"Yes it will, the legacy was a very generous one, and should even extend to little Jerome here." Father reached out to pat Jerome on the head. "The question is, will Luc extend himself to the legacy?"

"It's just that I don't want to go east until things are more settled here and our farm is secured," Luc tried hard to sound grown up and reasonable.

"As far as I'm concerned, things are settled. The people of Batoche have a legal claim to their land, even though the government in Ottawa is slow to recognize it. Nobody is going to take our land away from us. The sooner you and Jean and other young Métis learn the new ways, the better things will be. So you must carry on with your studies."

"But Père! The legacy money Monsieur MacDonald left you doesn't have to be spent on school. MacDonald was a trader and so were you. If Jean becomes a lawyer why not set me up as a trader or even as a farmer?"

Father raised his hand. "No. You need to get away from here. Go down east to learn. There'll be plenty of farmers left in Batoche and as I told you, the government won't interfere with our land rights."

"That may be true, Monsieur Goyette," said Pierre. "But Riel and the others are saying different. They feel that we can't trust the Canadians and that we must declare our own independence as a Mètis nation so that we can control our future."

Pierre leaned forward on his elbows and thrust his face toward Adrien. "They wish you would take a seat on the council when a provisional government is formed. Your advice is highly regarded."

Adrien's face flushed, anger crept into his voice.

"I can't support Riel anymore. He knows that. Yes, at first, I felt he was the man to speak for us to Ottawa, but now he goes too far. We can't just declare our own little kingdom. Louis Riel has a lunatic notion that he has some God-given right to rule. It's dangerous and foolish."

He paused to suck vigorously on his pipe; large clouds of smoke billowed from the glowing bowl. The muscles in his jaw twitched as he bit down hard on the pipe stem.

"I've seen the big cities in the east. We can't fight them. The days of the hunt and the old life are gone; we must adapt or be swallowed up."

Pierre leaned back in his chair, his eyes hovered sadly on the tin box. "*Nisitoothten*, Adrien. You may be right after all. My Mother's people won't change and they're almost starving this winter." He shook his head slowly. "Maybe we should move on, north and west. I don't know."

Luc gritted his teeth to keep from jumping into the argument. The old ways didn't have to die! Pierre's stories of hunting and freighting on the Carlton Trail with the Dumonts proved that. Who would be a boring lawyer when he could take to the prairie with horse and rifle? Riel was a lawyer and all he did was talk and shout at people. Isidore and Gabriel Dumont now — there were real men for you. They could ride, shoot, hunt, and fight better than anyone. But it was pointless to bicker with Father.

Pierre helped Luc finish his wood-splitting chores that afternoon before leaving. Luc swung the axe as hard as he could. The sweat steamed from his neck into the cold air. It was good to work off his frustrations and he felt better as they went through the low doorway into the poplar stick-barn.

Luc stroked the young mare's nose while Pierre hauled his saddle across the barn. "She's a beauty Pierre. I'll have one this spring."

"You've got horses," Pierre wrinkled his nose. "And three oxen that haven't been mucked out for a long time by the smell of it!"

Luc held the mare's head while Pierre threw the blanket and saddle on her back. "I mean a real horse, a pony like this. Not a work horse and certainly not an ox!"

"What will you really choose when the time comes, Luc? Will it be school and black-frocked priests in Montreal or the Saskatchewan Valley and the life of a Métis man?"

"I respect my father. He was one of the best traders in the Saskatchewan country twenty years ago. If he says the old ways must change, then I guess I can't argue, but still. . . ."

"That's your father talking." Pierre's voice was impatient. "He's a good man, I know that, but he has lost the Métis spirit."

Pierre tapped the side of his head with his finger.

"He's a farmer and a business man; he speaks French but he thinks English. If we don't protect the traditional Métis ways, then who will?"

"And that's the Dumonts talking! Yet I'll admit my heart is with you." Luc shrugged. "Anyway, I still have over a year before I'll be expected to make a choice."

"The choice may come sooner than you think, my friend."

The afternoon sun filtered through a crack in the barn wall behind Pierre. The weak light ringed him with a halo and cast a dark shadow over his face. Black paint on a Cree warrior's face meant only one thing. Death. A chill shivered down Luc's spine.

"What do you mean?"

"I didn't tell your father, but I can trust you," Pierre said in a low voice, looking suspiciously around the barn as though the animals might be spies. "Isidore Dumont has said that Riel wants to force a showdown. He wants to defy the Canadian government. Isidore says if it means we fight, then fight we will."

"Fight? What do you mean? Fight who, over what?"

"Well let's just say that if the Mounted Police try to interfere in our village they may find us difficult to subdue," hissed Pierre fiercely, his dark eyes flashing.

"You'll fight the Police? You can't! That's, that's just. . . ."

"Crazy?" Pierre grunted and spat. "You think Louis Riel is crazy, but he's not."

"When will you fight them? Do you have an ambush planned?"

Pierre led the horse out of the barn without replying and leaped up into the saddle like a cat. "I've said too much already, Luc. Forget it, you shouldn't become involved." He turned the pony's head and kicked her into a trot. The flashing hooves squirted up puffs of snow.

"Goodbye N'Sjayasis!"

Luc turned to trudge back to the house. The snow squeaked beneath his feet and his breath billowed in little clouds.

2.   Duck Lake

Luc was in high spirits. The day was fresh and mild for the middle of March. Sunlight sparkled on the snow that winter winds had drifted and packed hard. His snowshoes skimmed and slipped like skates on the crust. He had just checked the last of his traps and was climbing back up the small ravine away from the frozen river toward home.

The toboggan bounced over the snow behind him carrying its tiny cargo of one weasel, and a small one at that. It was all his traps had produced in six days. Perhaps he should move farther south or even across the river before it started to thaw. But surely he had enough fur already to get that pony, why move so late in the season? Pierre said prices would be good at Carlton this spring.

He shifted the old shotgun off his shoulder and cradled it under his arm. Maybe he wouldn't have enough for a rifle, but he'd get that pony for sure. It was on days like these that he felt sorry for poor Jean stuck in a stuffy old classroom cramming algebra or Latin into his head.

The thought was depressing. Would Father really make him follow Jean to Montreal? Did they all have to become lawyers and priests? Maybe Pierre was right. The Métis were the best soldiers on the plains. Surely they could fight to keep their land the way it was. Gabriel Dumont had once single-handed faced down a whole enemy war party.

He and Louis Marion were scouting the Blackfoot camp at night while the warriors danced and boasted of their victories over the Cree. Gabriel had leaped right into the dance and told them of the Blackfoot he had defeated. They were so impressed by his bravery that they had gone home without attacking any Cree villages.

But the Police were not the same as the Blackfoot. He knew several of the policemen. They often dropped in at the Goyette farm when out on patrol. They were big strapping men mounted on beautiful grain-fed horses. They wore handsome uniforms and had modern rifles. How could the Métis hope to fight them?

Luc's good spirits were dampened by these troublesome thoughts as he tramped the last half mile to home. He rounded the back of the barn.

"Ekwana, Atim! Let him be!"

The bellow came from the farmyard, the voice sounded familiar. Luc's stomach tightened to a knot. He kicked off his snowshoes and gripped the shotgun in both hands. He peered around the corner of the barn.

There were nearly a dozen mounted men clustered in front of the house. Two men stood at the door engaged in an argument with his father. They all carried rifles, except for one of the riders whose hands were tied behind his back. The prisoner shouted at his captors.

"Poltrons, he's unarmed!" The prisoner was Louis Marion, and he was being guarded by Edouard Dumont. But Luc couldn't worry about Marion, his eyes were drawn toward his father who looked so lonely among all the riders. Luc darted out from behind the barn and ran for the house.

As he got closer he recognized the men facing his father. They were Isidore Dumont and Pierre.

"Alright Goyette, follow your precious conscience." Isidore shook his fist. "But we will not forget who our enemies are!"

The burly Dumont turned abruptly and stamped down the path. Luc pushed by the horses and rushed forward to where Pierre stood talking earnestly to his father. Adrien Goyette was silent but Luc could see he was very upset.

Pierre was almost pleading, "Adrien, I'm speaking to you now as a long time friend. These men are serious; they are ready to fight, and they may not treat kindly those who refuse to support them. Please reconsider."

For an answer, Luc's father merely took Pierre's hand in his own, smiled and said, "You do what you

think is right, Pierre, and I'll do what I think is right. I
will not fight the police."

Pierre turned away. His face was taut with worry and
he glanced aside, avoiding Luc's eyes. He tried to brush
past, but Luc caught his arm.

"What's all this about, Pierre?" Luc whispered so the
other horsemen would not hear.

"It's a great day for the Métis nation, Luc. I only wish
you and your father could join us, but he is a stubborn
man. Yesterday, at Xavier Letendre's house, we formed
a provisional government and established the Métis
nation. Today we heard that the police are marching to
Batoche to arrest Louis Riel and Gabriel Dumont for
treason. We have gathered many men and we will fight
them!" Pierre slapped his hands together.

"Look there at Louis Marion!" Luc glanced back to
see Marion kicking at Edouard Dumont's horse. "He
refused to join us and he insults Riel. Calls him crazy.
We have arrested *him* for treason! That's why I am so
worried for your father."

Pierre slipped an arm around Luc's shoulders and
spoke quietly. "If he continues to stand by the priests and
the police he may be taken as a traitor as well. Talk to
him; urge him to reconsider. Riel respects your father —
he wants him to sit on the council. If he accepts, it will
be a great honour for the Goyette's and it will keep him
safe from some of the others."

He nodded at one of the riders who was shouting
curses and insults at Luc's father. Luc knew him, a bully

named Larouche. His huge body seemed to crush the sway-backed old horse he rode. Mother was always complaining about how he treated his daughter Marie. Although only thirteen, Marie worked at the Rectory, housekeeping for the priests. Mother said all of her wages went towards Larouche's drinking. He drank more than he worked and their farm was a poor one.

He was always rude to Father. On a buffalo hunt ten years ago Father had caught him stealing and had reported it to Gabriel. Larouche still held a grudge against the Goyettes.

"Take care N'Sjayasis!"

Pierre rushed to his horse, mounted quickly, and joined the others as they rode out of the farmyard. Luc's head was spinning; his father and the priests were supposed to be traitors? Louis Marion, a prisoner of a new provisional government, and more talk of fighting? His father whisked him inside where his mother waited fearfully with the two little children. "It's alright, everyone," said Adrien. "They're gone and we're safe."

"Père, what's going on? They've got Louis Marion. Pierre said you might be next!"

"They're fools," Father banged his fist on the kitchen table so loudly they all jumped. "They expect me to take an oath of allegiance to their tin-pot government. Anyone who doesn't is a traitor."

"What will we do if they come back?" The shotgun seemed to grow heavy in his hands. He looked at it.

Would he have to fight Pierre to protect his family? He couldn't!

"They won't be back Luc, they've got bigger plans right now. I'm just a minor nuisance." He laughed bitterly. "These idiots are planning to attack Fort Carlton, take the police there as prisoners, and then demand recognition from the real government in Ottawa."

"Oh, they are wicked!" said Luc's mother in a shocked voice. "Father Fourmond said it was a sin to take up arms in rebellion; they will commit their souls to the devil. And poor young Pierre with them." Her eyes were round with fear.

"If they think they'll win anything by starting a war now, they can think again." Father grabbed the shotgun from Luc and slapped the stock. "Most of them have nothing better than this old relic. I've seen the British army in Quebec. They will come in their thousands with cannon and torch to crush this little rebellion."

"Saint Peter preserve us!" Mother pulled her rosary from her skirt pocket and kissed it. "Adrien, what will become of us?"

Adrien forced a smile. He set the shotgun down and put his arms around her. "We'll be fine so long as we keep our heads, *Faon* . The army won't bother us, but you can pray for those hotheads because they'll surely be destroyed."

"Pierre says the Police are coming to arrest Riel and Gabriel for treason, but they've done nothing wrong!

That's not right, Père." Luc dropped his chin onto his chest and stared at the gun.

"Defending yourself isn't the same as rebellion is it?"

"Words, Luc! Just Riel's words to confuse things, and I *forbid* you to talk such nonsense."

Luc didn't look up, but he stubbornly refused to apologize. The kitchen was silent, even Jerome and Marguerite were quiet.

"Oh Luc." His father's voice softened. "I know how you feel, believe me I do."

He felt his father's hand rest gently on his shoulder. Looking up, Luc was shocked to see a tear in the corner of his eye.

"*N'Sjayasis*," his father sighed. "You're young and proud and loyal as a wolf."

Marguerite let out a squeaky howl that was abruptly stifled by her mother's hand. They all grinned with relief, the tension eased.

"I sat on the old council. I signed the petition to Ottawa and I was on the committee that asked Riel to come back to lead us! I want the same things as you and Pierre but we can't just start shooting Policemen if we don't get our way."

Luc's face burned. Father was faithful to the Métis cause. But still. . . .

"What if the police attack us?"

"Why then, young wolf, we fight back!" Adrien laughed and slapped him on the back. "But think, Luc.

Do you really believe Constable MacDowell and his friends would just ride into Batoche shooting people for no reason? Mon Dieu, they brought us medicine last winter when the influenza went through. Why would they attack us now?"

He shrugged. "It's just that Pierre made it sound a lot worse."

"He's been duped by Riel's quick tongue. Let's just hope he comes to his senses."

They ate a quiet dinner that night. Luc and his father did the chores in silence after supper; each seemed to be afraid to voice his worries. That evening he watched his father take the rifle down from the wall, check it carefully, and put it in the corner by the shotgun.

"Don't worry, son, I won't fight our friends however wrong I think they are. They are our people and will do us no harm."

There were riders on the trail to Batoche all that night and all the next morning, then it was quiet. Three days later the Goyettes ran out of tea, and then they used the last of their salt. They waited another full day before Luc hitched up the cutter and drove into the village with his father. They needed news almost as much as they needed salt.

The street in front of Letendre's store was frantic with activity. Young Indians were cantering up and down the street yelling and whooping. Métis men were jostling cutters and wagons, cursing each other to clear the road.

Some men hauled supplies into the store while others carried tools and equipment out.

There were at least fifty talking, laughing men, most of them armed, jammed inside the store. Adrien shouldered his way to the counter, Luc followed close behind. The shelves were nearly empty and Xavier Letendre was nowhere to be seen.

"Xavier!" Adrien shouted. "Batoche, where are you?"

"He's run off to Fort à la Corne! Who wants to know?" A rough voice bellowed in reply.

Luc froze, it was Larouche. The conversations gradually died out until the place was completely silent. Luc's father hurriedly picked up two items and left some money on the counter as payment. They turned to walk out when a tall, heavyset man stepped in front of the door, and raised his rifle threatening them. Larouche's cruel face, flushed with drink, looked down. Luc noticed Marie standing shyly in a corner. He caught her eye but she looked away, embarrassed.

The big man spoke, "What makes you think you can take supplies from the provisional government, Goyette? We're fighting a war of survival, we need everything for ourselves; there's nothing here for traitors."

Father stiffened, his face turned crimson. He replaced the items, and took his money off the counter.

"We'll go on to Duck Lake. Hillyard Mitchell's store is always well-stocked and he doesn't bully unarmed men and boys."

"Ha! That's funny. In a few moments we ride with Gabriel Dumont to capture the provisions in Mitchell's store and establish the provisional government in Duck Lake. Your Hillyard Mitchell will be wise to flee." Larouche laughed as though he had just told a great joke.

The other men laughed also, and it seemed to break the tension. Luc and his father hurried from the store. They were climbing into the cutter when Marie ran up to them.

"Luc, Monsieur Goyette," she called. "I'm sorry for my father's behaviour."

Father smiled at her. "Don't worry yourself, Marie. He hates me for something that happened a long time ago."

"Anyway," Marie continued, "I want you to have this, Luc." She darted forward and pressed a small leather object into his hand. It was a beautifully embroidered picture of a horse, delicately set against a pale blue background. Although small, it was perfect. He was about to protest that he couldn't accept it but she cut him short.

"Now you understand that some members of the Larouche family know their manners," she said defiantly. "Please say hello to your mother and the little ones for me." She ran down the snowy street and up the trail that led to her farm.

Luc's father winked. "She likes you that little one does, and she's pretty too!" Luc's face burned with embarrassment, but he secretly glowed with happiness.

The team pulled the cutter at a walk up the crowded street. Suddenly a great shout went up behind them.

"RIEL!"

Father reined in hard. Luc squirmed around on his seat to look back to Letendre's store. Louis Riel stood on the raised step and held a large wooden cross up high.

The crowd fell quiet. He began to speak but Luc couldn't hear the words. Those nearest Riel crossed themselves and bowed their heads. His eyes swept over them and for a second they glittered darkly at Luc. Luc's right hand moved automatically to make the sign of the cross.

A moment later Riel mounted his horse and was joined by the Dumont brothers. Gabriel stood up in his stirrups and thrust his rifle into the air.

"*Mes Amis!* The police march on Duck Lake. I am going to let *Le Petit* talk to them. Who will come with me?"

The men cheered and scrambled for their horses. Hundreds of riders clogged the street, following Gabriel. Pierre trotted right past the Goyette cutter. Luc caught his eye for an instant. Pierre grinned and said something to Isidore Dumont who waved. Luc waved back. Then they were gone, part of the river of Métis soldiers flowing down the trail to Duck Lake.

* * *

"It's war, boys! War, by God! They've gone too far this time and now we can teach 'em a lesson they'll never forget." Captain Lashbrooke was almost shouting with glee as he stamped his snowy boots on the doorstep. Tom's father showed the Captain into the house and closed the front door behind him. Lashbrooke was too excited to sit. He paced rapidly back and forth.

"The half-breeds on the Saskatchewan have taken these upstart ideas too far. Establishing a provisional government is one thing but taking up arms against Her Majesty, the Queen, is quite another! We're the lucky ones; our regiment has been called to mobilize. We'll join General Middleton and march on Duck Lake to crush these traitors."

He turned to Uncle Jim. "Colour Sergeant Kerslake, you are hereby appointed as Sergeant Major, G Company, Winnipeg Rifles, and called out on indefinite active service. Where is that bugler of mine, anyway?"

Tom had been standing just outside the room listening with growing excitement to the news. He stepped forward, trying to keep his voice steady.

"I'm here, Sir, and I'm ready to serve."

Captain Lashbrooke rushed to Tom's side, and slapped him on the back. "I knew I could depend on. . . ."

"NOW just hold yourself right there, Sir!" It was Tom's father. "You're not barging into my house and ordering my boy into any harebrained military adventure." He pulled Tom away from Lashbrooke and held him close.

"Explain yourself! What's all this about taking up arms?"

"The news came in this afternoon. I've been down at the drill hall getting my orders." The Captain's eyes glowed, and he gestured wildly with his arms.

"A column of Mounted Police met the insurgents at some place called Duck Lake and tried to stop them from ransacking the village. While they were parlaying under a flag of truce the devils opened fire from an ambush position and attacked our boys."

He pointed an imaginary gun at Jim. "The police returned fire and gave them a good thrashing but were forced to retreat as they were outnumbered. I'm sorry to say that many of our lads were killed, but the Winnipeg Rifles will avenge them, you may be certain of that."

He smacked a fist into the palm of his hand.

Tom's father looked pale. "Good Lord, I never thought they would actually fight. But surely we will call in the British Army regulars to deal with this?"

"We don't need the regulars," trumpeted an indignant Lashbrooke. "The Winnipeg Rifles can handle themselves. This is our party. One company is already assembled and will leave tonight on the train. The rest of us are to follow tomorrow when General Middleton arrives."

He turned to Uncle Jim and jabbed him in the chest with his finger. "Sergeant Major Kerslake here will be in charge of recruiting fifteen new men to bring my company up to strength before tomorrow. I'll need my bugler immediately; young Tom's skills will be indispensable in sounding the alarm."

He drew himself up to attention. "We could use men with your experience, George Kerslake. Why don't you join us, then you can look out for your son?"

"Don't be ridiculous, man," Father said with scorn. "I'll not quit my job to fly off with you on some goose chase, and neither will my son. He's in his last year of school and I will not have his education disrupted."

"Father, no!" Tom burst out. "I've been practicing my bugle for a month now, you have to let me go. Uncle Jim will be there and the rest of the company. They'll think I'm a coward if I stay back."

Father shook his head. "No! Not under any circumstance will you go off to this war."

Uncle Jim intervened. "Let the boy come with me tonight, George, he can help me with the new men.

Tomorrow's Friday; he can afford to miss one day of school, then I'll make sure he gets back home before we leave for the Saskatchewan country."

His father thought for a moment, indecisive.

"If you're set on this, Jim, I'll let him go with you to help out today. But he will never, I repeat never, be getting on that train." Tom's father glared sternly at Captain Lashbrooke.

Lashbrooke seemed not to hear him. He was already halfway out the door and merely called back over his shoulder, "Hurry yourselves! I'll gather the rest of the officers and meet you at the drill hall. Don't dawdle or you'll miss the picnic!"

Tom was upstairs in a flash, threw on his uniform, and clutching his bugle, came flying back down the stairs to find his father and his uncle in yet another argument.

"Party! Picnic!, the man's a bigger fool than I thought. You're not serious about going out to fight tough plainsmen in the middle of winter with a bunch of untrained clerks and boys are you, Jim?"

Uncle Jim replied patiently, "I'm a soldier, I gave my oath of loyalty to the Queen. We're Canadians now and it's my duty. I can't shirk it. Remember when we joined up in '62 with the old Wisconsins? I was only a boy then and we did alright at Shilo."

Tom's father spluttered with exasperation.

"Yes, of course, we did alright at Shilo, but we had six months training and were part of a proper army. Even then, we lost half of our regiment. This is a part-time army playing at soldier and you'll be up against men who have fought Indians and hunted all their lives. Look at what the Sioux did to Custer, and the Sioux are afraid of the half-breed!"

There was a long silence, then Uncle Jim simply said, "It's my duty. I'm going." He opened the door and let Tom go out first. Then as he was leaving, he turned back to Father. "Don't worry about young Tom. I'll have him back to you before we leave."

The rest of the day and well into the night were a blur to Tom. First they went to Uncle Jim's place where he made arrangements with his hired man to run the business and take care of the horses. Then it was back to the drill hall where a bubbling Captain Lashbrooke raced willy-nilly giving orders, shouting jokes to the men and generally getting everything confused. Uncle Jim quickly started organizing the company and soon had the men sorting out the stores, drawing weapons, and practicing their drill. Anyone without proper winter underwear, and socks, was sent home to get them.

Tom stood outside the drill hall and blew the assembly call over and over again. When his hands and trumpet got too cold to blow, he would come inside and one of the other companies would send their bugler out to take his place. They kept the clear, high-pitched assembly call going all afternoon and well into the night. Every hour more and more men answered the call.

Most were members of the regiment but many were new men who were quickly signed on and assigned to a company. In between his bugle duties Uncle Jim assigned him a recruit. Tom took the new man to the stores room where he drew a uniform. Then they went to the kit room where a huge tangled mound of knapsacks, belts, webbing, and even boots were heaped three feet high in the centre of the floor.

Tom pulled a cartridge box out of the tangle but it was so old the leather cracked when he opened it. The haversack they found stank and was slimy with mildew inside. The boots were twenty years old, neither Tom nor the recruit would even touch them. Eventually they found most of his equipment, but he wore his own shoes.

Nobody complained. Everyone was in top spirits and the fever of excitement, the new faces, the shouted orders, calling bugles, squads of drilling men, and general bustle were intoxicating.

When the first company marched down to the train station Tom ran along with them. They boarded the train at about nine o'clock that evening. The other men of the regiment, as well as several hundred townsfolk, were on hand to cheer them as they pulled out westbound. This was *his* regiment going off to war to save the country from rebellion. It was the biggest event of his life and he was going to miss out. All the other buglers were going, even Billy Buchanan over in "A" Company. He was only a year older than Tom, and not nearly as good on the bugle.

It was midnight before things died down. Most of the men either went home or slept on the drill hall floor. Tom found his Uncle in the company orderly room which was really just a table set up behind a blanket screen.

Uncle Jim looked exhausted but satisfied. "Well, not bad for one day's work, eh Tom, my boy? Look at this roll call. Fully up to strength; all men uniformed and armed. I hope we have a few days to do some drill and get some discipline established but they seem like good enough lads."

He tidied the papers away into a file.

"We can get to work on them tomorrow. I'll need you in the afternoon to teach the new men to recognize the basic calls. Right now, why don't you get off home to sleep?"

"Uncle J . . . uh, I mean Sergeant Major," Tom stammered. He braced himself to attention. "Do you think you could talk to father about me going west with the company? Everyone else is going and Captain Lashbrooke said we would be lucky to see any fighting. He thinks they won't have the nerve to stand up to us. I just don't see why I can't go."

"Tom, I gave your father my word I would see you home safe. You're only thirteen and whether we fight or not, a winter campaign is no place for a boy. I can't argue your case to him, I'm sorry."

Jim could see the disappointment on Tom's face and added, "I'll tell you one thing. If you were coming I'd be glad to have you in my company. You worked hard and did well today; I'm proud of you."

Tom blushed from the praise but it only made him feel more wretched. If the Sergeant Major thought he was a good bugler then that was all the more reason for him to go. There wasn't enough time to train a new man in his place. Tom put on his greatcoat and walked slowly out on to Hargreaves Street. A wagon had just backed up to the freight doors.

As Tom watched the men load it with boxes of biscuits an idea wormed its way into his head — a marvelous idea, the answer to his problems. Alone on the dark snowy streets he turned his idea over and over, refining it until by the time he reached home he had all the details calculated.

The next morning General Middleton arrived in Winnipeg and issued orders for the Rifles to leave that very day. There was a frantic last-minute rush to collect ammunition, food, stores and the piles of equipment required to support an army in the field. There was no bugle work for Tom as he was constantly racing about the drill hall or down to the train station on errands for Jim.

In the confusion of loading all the equipment onto the train, nobody was really watching too closely to see how things were stored, and that suited Tom's plan just right. Late in the afternoon Captain Lashbrooke sent Tom to see that his personal tent and equipment were properly loaded. The men on the work party were heaving Lashbrooke's gear into the boxcar any old way.

"Excuse me, Corporal," he interrupted the NCO in charge of the working party. "But Captain Lashbrooke told me to make sure his kit was properly loaded."

The Corporal, a man named Snell, threw Tom a nasty look. "Don't tell me how to do my job. Shove off!"

Tom took a step backwards and turned to leave. But if his plan was to succeed, he would *have* to get into the boxcar. It was that or be left behind. He worked up his courage, and turned back to face the surly Corporal.

"The Sergeant Major and the Captain both told me to come down here." He tried to sound forceful, and hoped mentioning the Sergeant Major would give him some authority.

Snell stopped work and stood, hands on hips, regarding Tom. The Corporal was a big man, nearly six feet tall and powerful. He was working in a light smock and trousers even though it was a cold day. The sweat from his neck and back steamed into the cold air.

"You're the Sergeant Major's nephew, aren't yuh, boy?"

"Yes, that's right."

"Yes, CORPORAL!" Snell barked. "You refer to me as Corporal."

"Yes, Corporal," Tom jumped to attention.

Snell smirked and picked up a large duffel bag. "Well
if the Captain sends his *pet* down here to load his gear,
then I guess you'd better load it!" The duffel bag hit Tom
in the chest. He found himself on his back, gasping for
air. Snell and the other men laughed, then went back to
work. Tom held his tongue; an argument now might ruin
his plan.

Captain Lashbrooke had a huge wooden steamer
trunk with iron straps around it, a large square canvas
bag containing his tent, and several wooden crates
marked fragile. Tom shifted the trunk and crates off to
one side and watched the men load the rest of the stores.
When the boxcar was nearly full, he grabbed one handle
of the big trunk and dragged it across the rough wooden
platform onto the boxcar.

The trunk was incredibly heavy, almost more than
Tom could move. By straining every muscle he finally
managed to shove it into position at a right angle to the
wall of the car and close beside the door. There was now
an empty space less than two feet wide between the trunk
and the jumble of stores in the rest of the car.

Moving quickly Tom piled the rest of Lashbrooke's
crates on top of and around the trunk so that the small
space was completely roofed over. Finally he took the
canvas tent bag and stuffed it up on end to cover the
entrance to his hiding space. Standing back he was
satisfied that nobody would spot the little room he had
just built. It was perfect for his plan to stowaway.

Tom got back to the drill hall in time to eat supper with the rest of the men before they marched down to the station. The scene at the huge CPR station was overwhelming. It looked as though the whole population of Winnipeg was on hand. The regimental band was on the platform playing one stirring tune after another and the crowd responded with even louder cheers.

Tom stood proudly to attention in front of G Company. The band struck up "British Grenadiers" and the people began to sing along.

"Of all the world's great heroes,

There's none that can compare,

A Tow row row tow row row

To the British Grenadiers."

The song finished with a roar that sent a shiver down Tom's spine.

"BATTALION!" Major Mackeand's command rang out. "Present Arms!"

Two hundred rifles smacked sharply into place. A short, corpulent man marched out of the station and onto the platform. He stopped facing the Regiment, directly opposite Tom.

"Men of the 90th Battalion!" The voice was power-ful, with a strong British accent. "Your Queen and your country are proud of you today."

The civilians cheered. The general took his cap off and waved it at them. His hair was wispy white. The tips of his walrus moustache stuck out past the bottom of his chin.

"The Winnipeg Rifles are a new regiment. But I know that if we meet the enemy, the Rifles will do their duty."

The general wore three medal ribbons on his dark blue coat. He was a brave soldier, but he looked older than Tom had imagined. His stomach strained against the sword belt. But that the sword scabbard was scratched and worn was good. Uncle Jim said the General had used that very sword in a desperate battle in India.

"God bless you all!"

Captain Lashbrooke leaped out in front of the Regiment. "90th Battalion! Three cheers for General Middleton!"

Tom's shout was one of the loudest.

"Hip Hip Hooray!"

The order was given to start boarding the train. Jim escorted Tom out of the ranks over to where Father and Vi were standing. Vi was waving a little Union Jack flag and calling out "Good Luck" and "God Bless" to the soldiers. Father flung his arms around Jim in a bear hug.

"Sure you won't change your mind and come with us?" Jim laughed.

"I can't afford to go play silly soldier when there's work to be done here," Father grinned. "Now don't do anything stupid. Take care of yourself."

Jim gave Tom a special hug then marched smartly to the train. Tom noticed that Vi had tears streaming down her cheeks. How foolish it was to cry at a happy time like this! But he couldn't stand around wiping Vi's tears; his time was running out. The men were almost on board the train. The crowd was so noisy that he had to yell to be heard.

"FATHER, I have to go back to the drill hall."

His father leaned close to him. "What's that, son? Aren't you going to see the men off?"

"Uncle Jim asked me to go back and clear away some of his reports before they close up the drill hall tonight. If I don't go now I may not get in." It had seemed like a good excuse when he thought it up and rehearsed it last night; now it sounded feeble. What if father simply told him to come home tonight and clear up the work tomorrow?

He didn't have to worry, Father wasn't suspicious. "All right son, but don't be late; you've been working hard these last two days."

Tom felt a pang of guilt. He was betraying his father's trust. Surely he owed his father the same loyalty as he owed the Regiment. The train whistle shrieked. He had no option, it was now or never. He ran off, weaving through the crowd down the length of the station and off the platform. He darted around the corner of the station to a bin full of brooms and shovels. He reached inside the bin and pulled his knapsack out from its hiding place, then raced off down the siding to his boxcar.

Disaster!

There had been a wooden ramp at the boxcar door when they were loading that afternoon. But now, of course, it was gone. There was no way he could reach up from the ground to the door handle. Even worse, it had been turned up into the shut position so that he would have to jump three feet into the air to grab it. In desperation he leapt and leapt again but didn't come close.

What a fool he had been not to foresee this! He looked quickly around, not even a crate or box to stand on. The engine at the front of the train gave a long blast on its whistle. It would move off any second now and leave him. Infuriated, he threw his knapsack to the ground and kicked it.

The knapsack, of course! It was a chance! He knelt beside the pack, pulled off his gloves, and began fumbling to loosen the buckle. The train suddenly lurched, all the cars clanging at their couplings as the engine took up the slack. Tom forced himself to stay calm and concentrate on the job of lengthening the strap. His fingers fought with the frozen webbing which was stiff and hard in the turn of the buckle. The train lurched again, moved several feet, then stopped. At last the buckle came loose and the strap flopped free.

Tom darted to the door, took aim and threw the knapsack up at the handle. It caught for an instant but the train jolted forward and the pack fell back down. The crowd at the station platform was in a frenzy of cheering. He glanced toward them, certain someone would see him. They were all concentrating on the passenger cars up front.

He retrieved the pack, flung it up, and this time it caught. The loose strap hung down only a foot above his head. He leaped, grabbed the dangling strap, and came down with all his force. Nothing happened. Frantic, he jumped up again, caught it and with a bang the handle shot down. He reached for the leading edge of the door, and hauled with all his might. The door slid back smoothly. Tom snatched up his pack but before he could pull himself up, the train began to move. He stepped back, ran two quick steps and launched himself at the partly open door.

He found himself on the floor of the boxcar with scarcely any room, the men had loaded it chock-full. Heaving on the door he rolled it back and slammed the handle up, locking it. He leaned back, panting, against the crates as the train picked up speed. He heard the crowd outside as his car passed the platform and he smiled to himself. If only Vi knew she was cheering her little brother off to war!

* * *

"It's beyond belief!" stormed Adrien Goyette. "You fools have plunged the Métis nation into an abyss." He hurled the pitchfork at the side of the horse stall with such force that it actually stuck, quivering in the wood.

Shaking a mittened fist at Pierre he went on. "To you this is some great adventure, but when the British Queen hears of this she will send her army to crush us and destroy our way of life. Leave this farm, I don't want to see you here again."

Pierre tried to explain. "But no, it was they who fired on us. They shot down Isidore in cold blood, what could. . . ."

"Neeak!" Adrien stamped past him out of the barn. Luc emptied a load of horse muck from the stall, then pried the pitchfork out of the wood. He could scarcely take in what Pierre had told them about the battle at Duck Lake. It overwhelmed his brain. It was crazy, like a bad dream.

"Is Isidore going to be all right? Was he hurt badly?"

Pierre looked grim. "Dead before he hit the ground, Luc. He and Aseeweyin, the old Cree chief, were talking to the policemen under a flag of truce. A flag of truce! I saw with my own eyes. The leader of the police had that cochon McKay with him as an interpreter. They ordered Isidore to clear the trail. The police wanted the supplies from Hillyard Mitchell's store in Duck Lake. When we refused to be bullied like children, McKay pulled his revolver and shot Isidore and Aseeweyin, both of them, at point blank range!"

Pierre pulled an imaginary gun from his belt and aimed it at Luc. "Two innocent men murdered!" He curled his lip and spat. "But I tell you, by heaven, we took our revenge. We had them surrounded, outnumbered, and caught in the open. We poured our rifle fire into them. They killed three more of our men with their first shots but then they ran like rabbits. We killed twelve of them and wounded many more."

Pierre rubbed one palm slowly across the other. "The trail back to Carlton was stained with their blood. We won a victory over these police. They are disgraced."

Luc could not believe his ears. "But your friend Isidore, dead?" Luc remembered the tough, burly man who had been so full of life and fire only a few days before, right here at the farm. It seemed so unreal that his life should be snuffed out.

"It's war, Luc! Some must die." Pierre was trying to sound hard, but Luc could see he was shaken. Even so, there was a confidence and fierce pride about Pierre that was exciting.

"What's your next move, Pierre?"

"The police have fled from Carlton and are holed up in Prince Albert. We'll wait to see what they do but should they venture out, we'll give them a hot reception. We'll need scouts, men who can speak English, and spies. That's one reason why I'm here."

He hesitated, looking back out the barn door toward the Goyette house.

"Can we count on you, at least, Luc?"

"You know how my father feels. I can't go against his wishes. You shouldn't even ask me Pierre. It's not fair."

"Was it fair when they shot down Isidore and old Aseeweyin?" Pierre snapped. "But there is a better reason for you to help us. Riel and Gabriel have heard how your father refused the oath. Now that it's war, they're determined to arrest him and even talk of confiscating the farm. If you don't join us and prove your loyalty to the Métis people, then it's prison for Adrien."

Prison! The word hit Luc like a punch. Could it be a bluff? No, he was certain Pierre was telling the truth. In fact, he suspected that Pierre had run some risk in coming to warn them. But Father would sooner go to jail than change his mind. Luc was caught squarely in the middle. He thought for a long moment, searching for an escape. There was none.

"I don't really have a choice, do I, Pierre?" He sighed heavily. "I'll do as you ask on condition that you never tell father. If you need me, come up from the river by the ravine. I'll make sure I'm out of the house every morning, noon and at sunset, to look for you. When the time comes for me to serve, I will tell father. But I won't worry him before it's necessary."

"Agreed, my friend," Pierre said with relief. "It's a wise and brave plan. Maybe they'll never ask for you. Just so long as I can reassure them that the Goyette family is willing to support the cause." Pierre shook his hand and turned to leave.

"Pierre," Luc called out. "If you come, I will do my best for the Métis Nation. You won't need to threaten me."

"Well spoken, Luc." Pierre climbed onto his horse and pulled a rifle out of the saddle scabbard. "I've got a new carbine, and a hundred rounds for it. We'll make the Policemen dance if they come after us again, eh?"

"Where'd you get it? Mitchell's store?"

"No, it was a gift!" Pierre laughed and slid the rifle back into the case. "It belonged to a Policeman, but he doesn't need it anymore."

Pierre dug in his heels and the mare shot out of the yard. He turned to wave, but Luc wasn't watching.

3.   The March

The candle flickered, guttered, then toppled over and went out. The boxcar was plunged into darkness. Tom fumbled along the floor, searching for the candle. The blackness was complete, unbroken by even the tiniest glimmer of light. He pulled a match from his coat pocket, and struck it against the rough crate. It flared brightly, revealing the candle where it lay at his feet. He picked it up, melted some wax from the bottom, and stuck it back on top of the crate. The tiny flame at least shed some light on his cramped hiding space. If only he could get some rest, some warmth.

The train swayed and rattled as it raced along the tracks, bouncing Tom around, making it impossible to sleep. His plan to stow away was not working out as he had expected.

He had hoped to pull several blankets out of Captain Lashbrooke's crates, wrap himself up in them, light a stout candle, and then rely on the blankets and the candle to warm up his hiding space. However there had been so many other crates and bags thrown in on top of Lashbrooke's things that he could not get at the blankets.

Then there had been his stupid move of leaving his gloves on the ground back at the station in Winnipeg. He was wrapped up in his own blanket, and had his candle going but there was precious little warmth to be had outside of the pale circle of light it cast. He hoped they would make good speed and reach their destination before he froze. Actually he wasn't certain what their destination was. Somewhere near the Qu'Appelle Valley he heard the Captain say, but where was the Qu'Appelle Valley? He huddled down to wait out the night.

The cold seeped through his clothes and began to cut into him. He tried stamping his feet to keep warm but there was no room. Soon he was so stiff and cold that he had to move. He crawled out of his hideaway and climbed onto the baggage. The dark closed around him like a shroud, everything he touched was covered in frost. He stretched his aching limbs quickly, then climbed back into his tiny room which at least had the candle light and a bit of warmth. He curled up — but he couldn't sleep.

The car rattled violently and his candle nearly fell over. Then the couplings clanged and the screech of brakes howled from the front of the train. At last! Eagerly, Tom climbed out and put his eye to a crack in the wall of the boxcar. He could just see the corner of a small CPR shack with a single lantern, no other buildings or lights were visible. Only a coal station; none of the troops were getting off the train. He went back to his cell.

The night was relentless, unending. They stopped again to let an eastbound freight train pass, then puffed slowly up to a cluster of dark sheds.

"All right 90th Battalion, everybody off!" Major Mackeand's voice roared over the hissing engine.

Tom snuffed his candle and groped through the dark to find the door handle. He grasped the icy latch and heaved it open.

"Listen Up! The CPR and the good citizens of Portage la Prairie have laid on a supper for us. You have one half hour to eat and stretch your legs. No man of the Rifles will leave the station without the permission of his company commander. Understood?"

Tom leaned out the door. The brightly lit platform far at the head of the train, was swarming with soldiers. A group of ladies waving Union Jacks stood by the station door.

"Welcome to Portage la Prairie!"

"God Speed, Boys!"

"Hurrah for the Winnipeg Rifles!"

Portage la Prairie! Not Qu'Appelle? Tom fancied he could smell the food and feel the warmth of the station. For a moment he was tempted to get down and join them. But the minute Uncle Jim spotted him, his soldier days would be over. He had to wait for Qu'Appelle. Miserable and lonely, he crawled back to his cramped space and with stiff fingers relit his candle. If only he could sleep. The eternity of the freezing night continued.

The clicking of the wheels slowed, or was it his imagination? No, they were definitely slowing down; the car jolted roughly as the braking engine sent its shock waves back down the length of the train. A feeble shaft of morning light slanted through the car roof. Tom stumbled from his tiny hiding space and peered through the gaps in the wooden siding of the boxcar. A sign crept past his car.

TROY.

The train shuddered, then stopped; all was quiet. Moments later he could hear the voices of the men as they unloaded. Just a rest stop, breakfast probably. Tom crawled back to his bleak homemade cave and curled up, determined to get some sleep now that the worst cold of the night was over. For some reason he felt quite comfortable and drowsy. He nearly succeeded in dozing off when the boxcar door suddenly crashed open.

"Right, step lively now, boys! We'll have these stores unloaded as quick as you can." It was Uncle Jim. Tom was up and out of his space like a gopher leaving its hole. The first men were already inside the car when Tom appeared.

"Well, look at this, it's the bugler!"

Tom scrambled past them and jumped down, stumbling to his knees in the snow. What a relief to finally get off the train. Jim stood a few feet away, staring at him in disbelief. Tom braced himself for the blast that was sure to come.

"Are you alright, boy?" Jim's voice was gentle. "You look half dead." Tom glanced down at himself. His rumpled overcoat was covered in dirt; his hands and face were blackened from huddling so close to the candle all night, and he was trembling from the cold and exhaustion.

He snapped to attention and tried to march to his uncle but his leg just crumpled and dumped him on the ground. There was no feeling in the left foot! It must have frozen overnight but he couldn't remember it going numb. Jim rushed over and scooped him up in his arms, walking quickly to a long shed near the tracks.

"It's alright, Uncle Jim! I'll be fine, I can walk," he said, ashamed to have the other men see the Sergeant Major carrying him like a baby.

"Don't tell me alright, you foolish young pup. Your face is frostbitten, one foot is gone and lord knows what else." Jim's voice was half angry and half worried. "It went down to twenty-two degrees below last night; it's a wonder you survived."

Tom touched his cheek and nose but felt nothing. Now he was worried. Twenty-two below! How could he have gotten so cold without noticing it? That sleepy feeling just when the train stopped. Of course! He'd heard lots of stories, growing up in Winnipeg winters. They said that freezing to death was a gentle way to die,

because you just lay down and went to sleep. He felt giddy
and was glad of Jim's support now.

Three stoves gushing heat marched down the centre
of the shed. They were flanked by rows of bunk beds.
Two soldiers were stuffing wood into the nearest stove.

"Get the doctor. Look sharp now!" Jim shouted. He
gently lowered Tom onto a bunk beside the stove. He
pulled Tom's heavy uniform off, and put extra socks on
his feet. He then got Tom curled up on the bunk and
covered him with a pile of blankets.

The doctor carefully examined Tom's hands, face
and feet. "It's not as bad as it could have been Sergeant
Major. He'll thaw well enough but it's going to hurt like
the devil," he clucked, shaking his head. Jim wrapped
Tom up again and told him to sleep. He could barely
utter a feeble "thank you" before his eyelids crashed shut
and he fell into a deep sleep.

He was standing in front of the stove at home in the
kitchen, holding out his hands to warm them. Vi was
cooking something that looked delicious. She warned
him not to get too close to the stove. The heat felt so good
that he moved closer anyway, but now it was too warm.
He tried to pull back but he couldn't. Soon his hands
and face were right up to the red hot stove and he still
couldn't force himself away from the heat that was
searing him. He called to Vi for help but she just ignored
him.

He woke with a start, but the burning continued,
even worse than the dream. He was drenched in sweat.

He could scarcely see. He tried to open his eyes wider but it was no use, he was looking through slits. He reached up to rub them and saw each finger on his hand was swollen up like a sausage. Now the pain really got bad.

The fire in his fingers was nearly more than he could bear. He writhed on the bed, wringing his hands as though he could shake the stabbing pain out. He sat up, jammed them under his armpits and squeezed, then pulled them back out and shook them. Nothing helped. Wriggling around, a new pain stabbed into his left foot. It seemed as though someone was sawing at each toe with a dull knife. Tears stung his eyes as he looked desperately about his bed for something to ease the agony.

There was a white enamel basin filled with water on a table in the centre of the shed. He rolled out of the bed but the first step on his left foot sent a bolt of pure flaming pain shooting up from the sole. He cried out and shifted onto his right foot. He hopped over to the bowl and thrust his hands into the water but there was no relief. Lurching and stumbling he made his way back to the bunk and collapsed.

He tossed and turned in a vain effort to escape the torment. Crazy images flashed through his mind; he could see the minister from their church and hear him preaching about the sins of the flesh. Unrepentant sinners were condemned to burn forever in hell. Frostbite was surely the devil's torture.

Hours passed with no relief. Where was his uncle, or the doctor; surely they could do something for him? The shed was empty; he was alone in a living nightmare. Just when he felt he could not stand another second, the stabbing pains in his foot began to dull. Soon his hands stopped shaking and then rapidly the burning died down to a slow throb. Tom exhaled shakily. He could feel his face cooling and he was able to control himself. He closed his eyes and lay back exhausted.

The shed door banged open.

"Well look here boys! The stow-away bugler has taken to his bed while we slave like coolies unloading stores!" The sneering voice was unmistakably Corporal Snell. Tom ignored him and kept his eyes closed.

"Thunder, look at his face and hands! He must have froze them solid," said one soldier. Tom heard them move close to his bunk.

"Is he dead?"

"No, you idiot."

"Well, the way he's swelled up — he sure looks dead."

"He's not a sideshow in a circus!" Uncle Jim's bellow interrupted them. "You men get on with your duties and leave him alone."

"Come on boys. Can't disturb the Sergeant Major's pet," Snell grunted. The solders scuttled out of the shed.

His uncle came to sit on the edge of the bunk.

"Where were you all this time, Uncle Jim? It hurt worse than anything I've ever felt."

"I know it's been bad, boy," Jim replied gently. "But I've only been away for about fifteen minutes. When I left you, you were sound asleep."

Fifteen minutes! Could that much pain have come and gone in such a short time? "It felt like forever, Jim. It felt like my hands were stuck in a fire."

"I know, lad." Jim felt his forehead. "You're lucky, no fever, so when the swelling goes down you'll be right as rain. Meantime you rest here; one of the orderlies will bring you some soup later."

Tom slept again, this time peacefully.

His hands and foot were still tender, but the swelling was nearly gone the next morning. It was time to be up and about his duties as bugler. Besides he was hungry for something more than the soup the medical orderlies had been feeding him. The rest of the men were already clearing out of the shed, heading for the cook's tent, and Tom hurried after them. Just as he was leaving the door the Sergeant Major's voice roared from the end of the building.

"Bugler Kerslake, you'll come with me now. You have an appointment with Captain Lashbrooke." Tom stopped short; Uncle Jim only called him "Bugler Kerslake" when he meant business. Moments later Tom stood to attention in front of the Captain. Lashbrooke's face was a bit puffy; Tom wondered if he had been caught in the cold himself.

"The bad conduct of any member of G Company reflects poorly on me," he began. Tom could smell rum

on his breath. "In particular, I expect those in positions
of responsibility to be scrupulous in their deportment.
This includes not only the officers and non-commis-
sioned officers, but my bugler. You are my voice in battle;
you are at my right hand." He raised his right fist like
a boxer. "Therefore your behaviour is a direct reflection
on my company and myself."

Tom's left foot was starting to throb; he hoped
Captain Lashbrooke wasn't going to get into one of his
long speeches about duty and honour. Besides, the reek
of alcohol on the Captain's breath was having a poor
effect on Tom's empty stomach.

"I'll come right to the point." Tom was relieved.
"The Sergeant Major here has recommended that you be
sent home directly by the next east bound train." Tom
was shocked. He had expected punishment but not to
be sent home in disgrace, and by his own uncle! He
turned to protest but Jim cut him off.

"You are standing to attention, Bugler Kerslake.
Look to your front and show some respect for the
officer," he barked.

Tom's face glowed red in embarrassment. He had
asked to be treated like a soldier; he should have known
better than to hope for special favours because his uncle
was the Sergeant Major. That was exactly what Snell
would have expected of him. He clamped his jaw shut,
determined to take his punishment without complaint.

"I am inclined to agree with the CSM," Lashbrooke
continued. "On the other hand, your youth and your

skill as a bugler are mitigating factors." Was mitigate good or bad? Tom felt it was a ray of hope.

"In fact you have become something of a celebrity in the regiment. The Colonel told me he admired your pluck. I told him that all my soldiers were very loyal to G Company." Captain Lashbrooke gave his huge mous-taches a self-satisfied twirl. "Anyway, after that I can hardly send you home." Tom was elated, but stood still, eyes fixed to the front.

"There must be punishment, however. I WILL maintain discipline. You will be assigned to perform company fatigues for the first week you are fit to return to duty. Carry on, Sergeant Major," he nodded to Uncle Jim who immediately marched Tom out. Tom wasn't certain what fatigues were, exactly. But it would have to be better than going home.

"Company! Officer on Parade DISMISS!"

Uncle Jim's command echoed across the parade ground. The men of Company G turned smartly to their right, lifted their rifles in unison, and slapped the stocks sharply in salute. A moment later, the three long ranks rippled as the men raised their right boots and stamped as one. Then the neat ranks disintegrated. The men shouldered their rifles and wandered off in small groups talking and laughing. The last drill period of the day was over early because Captain Lashbrooke was pleased with their performance.

The sun was still high in the western sky, and it sparkled on Tom's bugle. The snow and mud were gone.

If only he could go back to his tent and rest his aching foot. This would be a perfect day to clean his bedroll and blankets. But there was no rest for him. He had to run to his tent, change into coveralls, and report for fatigue punishments immediately.

"Kerslake!" barked Corporal Snell. "Move your idle frame. You report to me immediately after the day's drill is over, same as you've been doing for these last seven days. Even someone as stupid as you should know his duty by now!" As usual, Snell had several of his cronies nearby to laugh at his taunts. Obediently Tom ran over to where Snell stood.

"Bugler Kerslake reporting for fatigue duty," he rhymed off. "I was just going to change to my coveralls, Corporal." Tom's dislike of Snell put a hard edge on his voice. "The Captain ordered that I was not to ruin my uniform on fatigue duties."

Snell was furious. "Don't you dare talk back to me! You are an insubordinate piece of horse dung, Bugler Kerslake. I make the decisions around here. The captain and your precious uncle put ME in charge of your fatigue duties. I say you are late and must suffer the consequences. Now move yourself to the cook tent *on the double.*"

For the hundredth time that week Tom bemoaned his luck in being assigned to Corporal Snell. But he did not hesitate and ran straight to the cook's shack. The original punishment had been for one week and had started the day they marched north out of Troy to their present camp at Fort Qu'Appelle. That was exactly one week ago yesterday.

But Snell had been so obnoxious last evening that Tom had lost his temper and cursed the corporal. Snell had gleefully reported it to the Sergeant Major and as a result one further day's punishment had been awarded. If Tom could just keep his temper today, he would be free of his enemy.

The cooks had the usual duties for him. First he scraped out the grease and dirt left in the huge iron cauldrons used for the noon meal. Then he hauled water in two large wooden buckets, heated it in the cauldrons, and scrubbed them out. Next was the mountain of wood in the back of the cooks' tent. He had to split it to make the fires for the evening meal. Finally, he hauled the stew out to each company where the men waited in line, shouting at him to hurry.

When everyone else had eaten he was allowed to wolf down his own supper, standing beside the fire. Then it was haul more water, scrub out the cauldrons again and stack them away in the cooks' storage tent. By this time he was exhausted, but "the night was young" as Snell gleefully put it.

The minute the cooks released him he ran to Snell's tent where his tormentor had assembled all the boots, swords, and buckles from the company officers. Tom spent the remainder of the daylight hours sitting on a blanket in front of the tent, shining and polishing

the officers' gear. Snell passed the time insulting him and
criticising his work.

If only Vi could see him now! He would never ever
again complain about cleaning up a bit of mud from the
kitchen floor! When it was too dark to do any more
cleaning, one duty of the day remained. The senior
officers' horses were picketed to a rope outside the camp.
It was Tom's job to check them after dark, ensure they
were secure, and water them. This was one task he didn't
mind. Snell for some reason left him to do it alone, and
Tom enjoyed talking to the horses and stroking their
noses while he checked their lines. He didn't even mind
hauling the water.

Tom finished the last horse, took his lantern and
turned back toward the camp. He hadn't gone five paces
when a figure leaped out from behind one of the horses.

"Stop where you are, Bugler Kerslake. Come here."
Tom could see two of Snell's buddies standing back in
the shadows near the horses. He hobbled over as fast as
his aching foot would carry him. He was taking no
chances this close to the end of his fatigues. Nothing
Snell could say would get to him.

The Corporal looked him over carefully in the dim
light of the lantern. "Why you're filthy, Bugler Kerslake;
your best uniform is a disgrace. You should have changed
it before coming onto fatigues duty." The audience
snickered behind Tom's back.

"You ordered me to do fatigues in my uniform,
Corporal." Tom kept his voice steady.

Snell only smiled. "Are you suggesting that I would alter one of Captain Lashbrooke's orders? No! No! Oh no! You're mistaken. You're such a stupid little bugler that you forgot to change, isn't that right?"

"Whatever you say, Corporal." Tom was too tired to care about such insults.

Snell put one hand on Tom's shoulder as though to brush off some dirt; then suddenly gave him a quick shove. Tom stumbled backward, his heels caught against one of the bullies, and he went down arms flailing. The stink of fresh horse manure was overpowering. The smelly muck was smeared all over the back of his uniform jacket. He lay winded while Snell and his buddies walked away whooping laughter. The urge to chase them, to scream at them, was almost overpowering. But Tom controlled himself and merely got to his feet and trudged back to camp.

How would he wash his uniform and find some way of drying it before the morning reveille call? He changed into his coveralls and began to scrub the tunic with a stiff brush and soapy water. The other men in the tent were already settling into their blankets for the night, so Tom moved outside and worked by the faint glow of the lantern.

It seemed army life consisted of nothing but hours and hours of boring drill, dirty jobs, cold tents, and tasteless food. Where was the glorious battle? The rebels would likely just give up the fight and go home out of sheer boredom if they waited for General Middleton to do anything. A footstep sounded in the dark. Tom looked up to see his uncle approaching. He sprang to attention.

"It's alright, Tom, keep working. I've just come for a visit. So, is the soldier's life as exciting as you thought it would be?" His uncle laughed. It was the first time since Troy that Jim had called him by his first name or even been friendly to him. Tom felt a surge of relief, as though he had finally managed to climb some huge hurdle and was now safely over.

"Not much glory for me, Sir." He slopped a load of water onto a large yellow stain and scrubbed hard. "The boys in the tent say we'll never get to fight if we spend all our time on drill."

"So the boys are all military geniuses after one week of soldiering, are they?" Jim laughed again. "As a matter of fact, you'll be awakened an hour early tomorrow to blow reveille. We march north for the rebel capital."

"That's the best news I've heard all week!"

Jim's smile faded and his voice was serious. "I'm against it myself. These men are good lads but they're not soldiers yet by any stretch of the imagination. If Dumont fights, and I'm sure he will, he'll make short work of our lot."

Tom stopped scrubbing. How could his uncle think the regiment wouldn't fight? "But the Captain himself said our drill was near perfect today, even the general complimented us."

"Tom, good drill doesn't replace discipline, and discipline wins battles. Standing to attention on a parade square is one thing. Standing fast while your friends are being blown to pieces all around you is another."

He tapped the bucket of soapy water with the toe of his boot. "Why you're probably the only soldier in G Company who actually does what he's told without question. It wouldn't hurt all of them to spend a week at fatigues under Corporal Snell."

"But Snell is a bully and a cheat!" Tom burst out before he could stop himself. He couldn't let his uncle think of Snell as a good soldier.

"He is to you, Tom. But do you think those buffalo hunters are going to handle us with kid gloves? Just spend half an hour with one of them shooting at you, my boy, and you'll be wishing you were back scrubbing out the cauldrons."

With that he got up and moved off into the dark. He was a different man from the happy-go-lucky uncle back in Winnipeg. Tom rinsed his uniform, hung it over a tent rope, and rolled up in his blankets to sleep.

They were up by six A.M. and the whole camp buzzed with activity. Tom, happy just to be off fatigues, spent the morning racing to and fro carrying messages for Captain Lashbrooke. All the men joked and laughed. They were eager to go. At first the soldiers milled around in cheerful confusion but eventually the tents were struck, and provisions were packed. They started the march at noon.

The north slope of the valley was steep. Two of the wagons got stuck and the men had to pull them out of the mud. Up on the flat prairie above the river valley a cold wind struck head on. The wind brought a heavy rain that soaked them. Then the rain changed to sleet.

Tom marched at the head of G Company beside Captain Lashbrooke. The wind whipped stinging sleet into his face. Each step was an effort in the sticky, ankle-deep mud. They always seemed to be falling behind E Company. Every few minutes one of the General's aides would gallop down the line and shout. "The General's compliments, and would you please close up, Captain?"

Lashbrooke would curse and fume but soon Uncle Jim's voice would bellow out from the end of the column, "Double time, G Company!" Every soldier then groaned loudly before breaking into a run.

The sullen clouds stretched from one horizon to the other, and the north wind lashed the barren prairie. The line of dark green soldiers crept like a worm inching across a great muddy plate. At long last a halt was called. Tom, nearly soaked through with the freezing rain, merely found a grassy patch of ground out of the mud and flopped down. His left foot was pounding, they must have covered twenty miles.

"Captain Lashbrooke!" The General's aide trotted up on his horse. "We'll make camp here. Warn your men that we will have to do better tomorrow. We only managed ten miles today."

Do better tomorrow! Tom kicked his boot off and began to massage his foot.

"On your feet, you idle boy!" It was Snell, full of energy and not affected at all by the long march or cold weather. "What a sad lot you are." He was shouting at all the men in Tom's group. "Get your tent up, smartly now. Let's see you move!"

The wild wind knocked their tent down three times before they finally got it to stay up. They stowed their packs inside and made for the cook's wagon. To their dismay, the cooks had only built a small fire to boil some tea, no hot food. There wasn't enough wood for a proper cooking fire. Tom stood shivering by the puny fire as he sipped his tea and gnawed the hardtack biscuit.

By then it was late and growing dark. The sentries were told off for the night and the rest returned to the tent to roll up in their blankets on the sodden ground.

The wet canvas bell tent stank. The other men were black lumps, scarcely visible in the last dim light of the day. Tom snuggled down into his damp bed, wriggling to find a smooth patch on the lumpy ground. Eventually he got comfortable and curled up. His body soon warmed the blankets and he began to doze.

"Young Kerslake! Are you there boyo?" The strong Irish voice interrupted Tom's attempt at sleep.

Tom smiled; Patrick Flaherty was the comedian of their little group. He always had a joke to tell or "advice" to give. "Yes, I'm here, Paddy," he answered.

"I've some advice for ye then. Listen carefully to your old friend Paddy." A few of the men chuckled. "I've just got me old Irish bones nice and warm and comfy. I do not intend to stir meself until I've had at least ten hours of sleep. So you just keep that bugle of yours quiet tomorrow morning."

"I'll be quiet as a mouse, Paddy," Tom answered. "Just for you."

"Aye, yer a good lad and all, Tommy."

They slept.

Tom was already awake, teeth chattering, when the sentry came to get him. He dragged himself out of the blankets and stood in his stockinged feet searching for his clothes. He found them not only wet but stiff with frost. The touch of the damp clothes was revolting but his body thawed them once he had his great coat on, even though it, too, was only partly dry. His boots were another story. They had frozen solid as stones overnight. He grabbed the tent peg mallet and pounded them until they cracked open enough to fit his feet.

The rain and sleet had stopped but all the puddles were frozen. The grey dawn light revealed a few others stirring. His uncle was already up and bustling around supervising the cooks who were getting the morning tea ready; no hot breakfast for them today.

Tom dug the trumpet mouthpiece from his pocket, warmed it under his armpit for a moment, then inserted it into the bugle. He took a huge breath, let half out, and blew the reveille call. The clear, piercing notes of the bugle never failed to rouse Tom. This morning was no exception and he was soon putting everything he had into the sharp, strident wake-up call that echoed through the tents of sleeping G Company. He was glad to see that Snell looked particularly groggy and uncomfortable when he struggled out of his tent.

This morning they packed their gear much more quickly, gulped a mug of tea, ate a biscuit and were marching by eight o'clock. Tom's left foot ached with each step. As the day warmed, the trail melted and turned to the same sticky, ankle-deep mud. Tom felt he was on a treadmill, the horizon never came closer— just endless flat prairie. The line of soldiers followed the narrow trail as it dribbled around sloughs and past the odd clump of willow bushes.

Noon came and went; still they marched. The afternoon wore on, Tom gave up hoping for lunch and just concentrated on the man in front of him. The men were now so tired that they had even stopped grumbling. The only sound was the occasional grunt or curse as someone slipped in the mud. Lashbrooke muttered and complained because he didn't have a horse. But the Captain was careful not to say anything when the General happened to ride nearby.

It was four o'clock when they finally stopped. Uncle Jim told him they had covered only fifteen miles. Tom could scarcely muster the strength to chew his hardtack biscuit, much less imagine marching farther tomorrow. They finished their supper and went to get their tent from the wagon.

"G Company!" The Sergeant Major's command stopped them. "Fall in, column 'o fours."

"Oh my sainted aunt! We're not marching again?"

"Yes we are, Patrick Flaherty, and you can be right marker as a treat." Jim's voice was chirpy and bright. "Come on lads, the General only wants another five miles."

The men were furious but soon they were back on the trail. Tom wondered about soldiering as they plodded off again. It was certainly different from what he had expected.

The next day's march was even longer and muddier. At the end of it Tom sat cross-legged near his tent. He had removed his left boot and was massaging his sore foot. The tenderness from the frostbite still lingered. The marching had chafed off pieces of dead skin and replaced them with blisters.

"How's the foot?"

Tom looked up to see his uncle approaching.

"Oh, not as bad as last week — it's getting better," he lied, putting his boot back on.

"I saw you limping today," Jim said quietly. "I can get you a seat on one of the wagons if you like."

"No! Thanks anyway, but I'll be fine. My place is with the Company, I don't want any special favours."

His uncle smiled. "You're turning into a real soldier, Tom."

Tom said nothing but he could feel the pride well up inside.

"Come on, I'll show you some professionals, the Montreal Artillery are coming into camp."

He followed his uncle to the edge of the 90th Winnipeg Rifles camp. A crowd of men were standing beside the trail watching a column approach from the south. The General was nearby on his horse. Leading the parade were two trains of horses, each hauling a cannon and its limber. Fifty soldiers followed, marching in perfect step. Their uniforms were dark blue, and impeccable. Each rifle was carried at the correct angle and the soldiers stared straight to their front as they marched along. The cannon barrels glistened in the setting sun and the artillerymen sat calmly on small leather seats atop the limbers.

As they neared the General, the Artillery officer executed a very smart salute, flourishing his sword in a wide arc. The men of the 90th cheered them three times over. The officer gallantly tipped his cap in reply. They wheeled off the trail and broke ranks. Each man seemed to know exactly what was expected of him so that in a matter of minutes they had raised their tents, unlimbered the guns, and picketed their horses. Tom was impressed. It felt good to have regular soldiers in camp.

The trek continued. Each day they had to be up earlier, hike farther and move faster. The trail took them north, through the Touchwood Hills to the edge of the

Great Salt Plain, near two huge sloughs called the Quill Lakes.

"Fifty-five miles, alkaline water, and no wood." The Sergeant Major paused to let the words sink in. G Company sat in a semicircle, Captain Lashbrooke and Uncle Jim stood in the centre.

"The General proposes to cross the Great Salt Plain in two days. It will test us." The Captain spoke now, pacing back and forth. "But G Company will be equal to that test. We will show the same dash and. . . ."

Nearly thirty miles a day! No fires and only what water they could carry! Tom rubbed his foot. Could he do it?

"All of Canada is depending on us; watching us. We will not fail them, nor. . . ."

Paddy Flaherty sat next to Tom, his pipe belching clouds of smoke. Paddy's face was brown and hard as tree bark. They were different from the men that had left Winnipeg just three weeks ago. Tougher for sure, but something else too. Was it discipline? Friendship? Tom couldn't name it but he could feel it.

"No man from Company G will fall out of tomorrow's march."

Uncle Jim's lean figure stood in front of them. His voice was calm. "No stragglers. No excuses. No weaklings. During the next two days you will prove to me that you are soldiers. Now get some sleep, we start early."

The men broke up quietly and drifted back to their tents.

Tom staggered and grabbed desperately at Captain Lashbrooke's arm to keep from falling.

"Unhand me! You'll knock us both into the drink you young fool."

Tom heaved his foot clear of the gluey mud and splashed forward. The stream was only a few feet wide and six inches deep at the ford. But the horses, mules, wagons, cannons and two hundred men that had crossed before him had left a mud hole over a foot deep and twenty yards across. He plunged recklessly ahead and made it to dry ground, panting.

"Don't stop — Close up — close up." Jim nagged them. "Double time G Company! Let's go!"

Tom trotted forward, water and mud squelching out the tops of his boots. A half mile up, he could see a narrow ditch cutting across the trail. Another stream! The artillerymen were already bawling at their horses to "git-up" as they dragged the heavy cannons through it.

"Jasuz, Tom!" Flaherty's voice gasped for air. "D'ye think we've proved ourselves to your uncle yet?"

"Almost half- way, Patrick."

"Oh, thanks for telling me that, Thomas." Flaherty wiped the mud off his rifle as they jogged. "I'd hate to think all this fun was coming to an end."

They camped two nights later at the village of Humboldt. The word "village" was an exaggeration. It was really just a couple of shacks and a telegraph station. But the ground was dry, the water was clean, and there was plenty of wood. Even better, they had hot stew for supper. The stale old hardtack almost tasted good.

The air grew chill, but the sky was clear and the sunset was a blaze of scarlet and pink in the western sky. The boys had lit a fire and were clustered around it singing.

"Tommy, come and join us!" Patrick Flaherty beckoned him. The flames from the bonfire leaped five feet into the air but there was plenty of wood, so the boys piled it up high. Tom squatted in the circle of men, the heat scorched his face. A new song was struck up, "The British Grenadiers", and Flaherty led them through it.

"Well sung lads!" Tom peered past the sparking fire into the night to see Captain Lashbrooke standing just outside their circle. He stepped past the men and into the light. "But listen, we don't need the British Grenadiers! The 90th Battalion, Winnipeg Rifles are more than a match for these rebels. We march tomorrow for Clark's Crossing and enemy territory."

The boys cheered. Lashbrooke smiled broadly and raised his hand for quiet. "And be sure of this, if there is a chance for glory — G Company will be first in line!"

Another cheer went up.

"Now the Sergeant Major has something for you."

Uncle Jim appeared carrying a small wooden keg. He set it in front of Flaherty.

"I found no stragglers. I saw no weaklings. And I heard no excuses. I'm proud of you boys." He winked at Tom. "I mean, I'm proud of my soldiers!" He pointed at the keg. "This is the last barrel of syrup in Humboldt — I trust Private Flaherty will give everyone an equal share."

Tom went first. There was no attempt at good manners. He poured the sweet sticky stuff over his biscuit and crammed the whole thing into his mouth at once.

4. Spies at the Crossing

Jerome! Leave those birds alone. They won't lay a single egg now!"

Jerome ignored the warning and charged yelling into a cluster of hens. The chickens exploded, squawking in all directions.

"Jerome!" Luc slammed the barn door and sprinted across the farmyard. His little brother gave a yelp of alarm and took off past the root cellar, toward the ravine. Luc caught up to him at the edge of the trees and grabbed him by the back of the neck.

"Petit Diable! How many times have I told you to. . . ."

Two men stood just inside the poplar bluff at the crest of the coulee. They both carried rifles. Luc twirled Jerome around and swatted his bottom.

"Go into the house, hurry. And stay there."

Jerome was gone like a tiny rocket. Pierre pushed through the trees, his carbine cradled loosely in one arm. Larouche stayed back in the bush, scowling as usual.

"It's good to see you again, Luc. How's the family?" said Pierre as he shook Luc's hand and smiled warmly.

"We're fine. No news from Jean of course since the fighting, and mother is upset because she hasn't been to church in two weeks, but we're alright." Luc refused even to glance in Larouche's direction.

"Get to the point, Gladieu! Ask the boy if he will do the job or not. I have my duty to perform," growled Larouche.

"It is time, my friend. The soldiers have passed through Humboldt and are now at Clark's Crossing. We have a spy in their column but we need to scout their camp and we have to contact our man for information. We need someone who can speak English, knows the crossing, and will not be suspected." He placed his hand on Luc's shoulder.

"You are the perfect choice; Gabriel Dumont himself suggested your name."

He nodded toward Larouche. "If you don't agree to do this job, then . . . uh." Pierre's face flushed and he fiddled with the sling swivel on his rifle. "I'm sorry Luc. I hoped we could leave you out of it. But if you don't come, well . . . eh bien," Pierre shrugged helplessly.

"What he's trying to say Goyette," Larouche bulled his way forward through the trees. "If you don't come, then I arrest your father as a traitor."

"You don't need to threaten me, Monsieur Larouche." Luc stared Larouche in the eye. "I'll tell my father and be ready to go within an hour."

Larouche actually looked disappointed, but he said nothing. "I told them you would uphold the Goyette name." Pierre laughed with relief. "I'll wait outside the house."

Luc's mother was in the kitchen, dabbing tears from her eyes while his father comforted her. "So they've come at last, have they?" his father asked.

"It's alright Father. It's me they have come to see, not you," Luc answered. "I have decided to fight for the Métis people. I think it's my duty."

"DUTY!" his father exploded. "You're fourteen years old boy! Your duty is to obey your father. Those fools will ruin all that we hope to achieve as a people. They'll destroy us with this war."

Luc said nothing.

"Can you honestly stand there and tell me that you feel more loyalty to *ce chien*, Larouche, than you do to me?"

Luc shook his head no and looked down at his feet, ashamed that his father should think he held Larouche in any respect at all. But what could he say?

His father was silent, staring at him as though he could read Luc's mind. He snapped, "They're forcing you to go. It's me they want really, isn't it, Luc? It's Larouche trying to get revenge on me by forcing you to go fight."

Something stirred in Luc. Nobody was going to call him Larouche's puppet. Nobody!

"No, Father, you're wrong this time," he answered quietly but firmly. His mother sniffed and wiped her eyes. "I'm not like Jean. I'm not a student or a lawyer or a priest. I'm Métis! I love our farm, and hunting in the valley, and our family. I'm not fighting for Larouche but for us and our home here on the Saskatchewan."

He looked up and met his father's eye.

"I know," his father sighed. "I guess I knew from the night we got news of the fighting at Duck Lake that you would go with them. After all, you are part Cree and that warrior blood seems to flow strongly in your veins. I might have done the same thing when I was your age."

His father went to the fireplace and took down the rifle. He gave it to Luc, held him in a powerful hug, then left the house, all without a word.

"Luc, you know what the priests said." His mother's voice quivered, she was almost crying again. "You must not fight the police."

"Jerome! Guess what?" Margeurite ran from the kitchen and climbed the stairs to the bedrooms. "Luc's going to shoot a Policeman! Bang! Bang!"

That was the last straw. Mother burst into tears and rushed to Luc. He held her tightly.

"It's not like that. . . ." A huge lump choked his throat. He swallowed and tried again. "I won't hurt anyone, Mama. They just need me to speak English. Maybe a little scouting; talk to the soldiers. That's all."

Strictly speaking he was telling the truth. But he clutched the rifle in one hand, and they both knew what might happen. She gulped a sob and stood back wiping her eyes.

"*Petit oie*," she managed a weak grin. "It's you I'm worried about, not the police. Now go, I'll pack some things. Leave before my heart breaks." She lifted her small silver crucifix to her lips. Luc bolted for the door before he lost his nerve.

His father was outside talking to Pierre. Larouche waited back at the edge of the ravine. "I still can't agree with what you are doing, Luc, but I am proud of you." Père put his arm around Luc's shoulders and squeezed him.

"Pierre has told me that they will want you to do some scouting. Please, for God's sake, don't take any foolish chances and remember that scouting is like hunting. Observe and be patient, let your prey do the moving, let him make the mistakes. You stay under cover."

Father hung a brass powder flask around Luc's neck and handed him the leather bag that contained the percussion caps and bullets for the rifle. Luc grabbed Pierre's outstretched hand and swung up behind him. The pony skittered under the extra weight.

"I'll be careful, Father. Besides, Pierre says that after Duck Lake the Police are afraid to come out to fight us. There's no real danger."

"You're wrong, Pierre." Father's voice was grave. "There *will* be fighting. These soldiers haven't marched two thousand miles in order to surrender. I'll pray to God to protect both of you."

Jerome emerged from the house lugging a bedroll. "Mama says there's socks, a shirt, and moccasins inside." He struggled to lift it up onto the saddle. "Oh yeah, and she said she loves you."

Luc sat with Pierre in the back room at Batoche's store that night. Neither spoke, they waited in silence. The lamp on the table shed a puddle of fluttering light on the floor between them. The door opened and a short, muscular man entered the room. A thirteen-shot Henry repeating rifle was balanced casually in one hand. Gabriel Dumont turned to look directly at Luc. His dark eyes were like lit coals in the dim room. They seemed to burn right through him.

"*Mes Éclaireurs,*" he grunted. He laid his rifle on the table, the lamplight glinted from its polished brass receiver.

"The soldiers have been at Clark's Crossing now for five days. I have a spy working as a teamster for them, and I have Gilbert Breland watching the camp. You will ride from here at first light tomorrow and approach their camp after dark."

He paused, scratching gingerly at a long gouge on the top of his head. It was partly healed, partly raw. "A present from a policeman's gun at Duck Lake," he explained.

"Young Goyette, you must get into the camp, meet my man, take a message from him, and give it to Gilbert Breland. He will bring it back to me. You two will take Breland's place for the next couple of days, stay concealed, and watch the enemy camp. If they move, one of you will ride back to tell me, the other will stay to trail the soldiers. Questions?"

"Yes," asked Pierre. "How will we find Breland?"

Dumont chuckled, "Don't fear, he'll find you. You can easily avoid the clumsy soldiers but you will never approach Clark's Crossing without Gilbert spotting you. The man you will meet inside the soldiers' camp is Jerome Henry. You will not be able to creep into the camp by stealth. You must be bold." He rapped the table sharply with his fist.

"Wait until dark, then go unarmed. Approach the main sentries, tell them that you have an important message for Jerome Henry. Use your best English. They'll never suspect an English-speaking boy and anyway, there are people coming and going from the wagon lines all the time. When you find Henry, tell him you have a message from Antoine de Padoue. That is important, Antoine de Padoue. He will slip you the information I need."

Dumont gripped Luc's shoulder, and smiled. "*Eh bien, jeune chasseur* it will require nerve, but you are the son of a brave man. I know you will not fail."

Luc flushed with pride — a great compliment from the bravest of them all, Gabriel Dumont. Yet Gabriel had also sent Larouche to arrest Father. What kind of compliment was that?

"Never fear, *mes amis*, this will be just like hunting buffalo again. What could be more exciting, eh?"

They laughed — Luc loudest of all.

They were on the trail from Batoche heading south to the Crossing before sunrise. Gabriel had borrowed one of the Nault's ponies for Luc, so they made good time. As they approached to within a few miles of Clark's Crossing, Pierre became very careful and slowed the pace. Though there was no sign of the soldiers he kept his eyes constantly on the horizon. Every time they came to a slight rise he would stop to study the ground ahead of them before they continued.

When they were still about four miles from the crossing they turned right, off the trail, and headed for the River. They dismounted and led the horses down the steep embankment to the water's edge where they rode on for about another mile, carefully picking their way along the shoreline. Reaching a small patch of trees they unsaddled the horses, fed and watered them. They led the horses into the woods and tethered them out of sight.

"From now on, Luc, we go quietly. We'll be concealed but the soldiers may have sentries on the top of the banks, so we must not let them hear us."

Pierre sounded so calm. Luc could scarce keep his teeth from chattering. They moved cautiously along the river, hugging the tall embankments until they drew near the crossing. The bank dipped down to the water level

where a small creek, trickling to join the river, had cut a
ravine in the prairie. The ravine itself was choked with
poplar brush.

They began to climb back up toward the higher
ground. The sun was just beginning to set; it was already
dark in the wooded bottom of the coulee. They chose
each step carefully and paused often to listen. Suddenly
Pierre stopped and stood rock-still. Luc froze. He heard
nothing, saw nothing. Pierre began sniffing the air like
a dog.

"Do you smell them, my friend?" Pierre whispered.
Luc smelled nothing, he shook his head. "Try again! Use
every sense, not only your eyes and ears. Close your eyes,
you must feel what is out of place to know when danger
is near."

Luc closed his eyes and frowned in concentration.
He could smell the damp from the tiny trickle of creek
water and the closeness of the rotting leaves and undergrowth. He could even smell the cooling of the air as the
evening frost began to settle. Then he had it, an unnatural smell among the natural. It was faint, but distinct
— the smell of wood smoke, meat burning or cooking.
"Cooking fires," he whispered. Pierre grinned and
nodded. He pointed to the top of the ravine and began
to move up.

The rim of the coulee was only thirty feet above the
creek bed but it took nearly ten minutes to creep up level
with the prairie. The view at the top astonished Luc.
There, not half a mile away, was the river— between them

and it was the soldiers' camp. Rows and rows of white bell-shaped tents, neatly laid out in little streets running back from the crossing. Dozens of campfires sparkled in the gathering dusk.

Luc looked with admiration at Pierre. He had led them nearly to the enemy's doorstep without being discovered. Their position here was perfect. They could lie at the edge of the ravine, observe all that went on, and if need be escape back down the creek bed undetected.

Pierre pointed out the lines of wagons and tents where the teamsters were camped. He also nodded to where the main trail approached the crossing. As they lay quietly studying the enemy tent lines, Luc rehearsed for the hundredth time what he would say when he entered the camp. The thought filled him with dread and excitement. What a story he would have to tell them back at Batoche! Then Larouche would have to watch his tongue when he spoke about the Goyettes.

Presently they slid back down into the trees. Taking bread and dried meat out of their bags they ate in silence. Luc was too nervous to be hungry but he had to eat to stay strong. He might need all his energy if they were forced to run for it.

He finished his food and lay back, gazing at the first stars to appear in the darkening sky. The trees were still bare; it was easy to pick out the Big Dipper and the North Star. There was a thin sliver of crescent moon which gave a faint glow of light. *Niskapesim!* One of the trees swayed slightly in the evening breeze. He loved this beautiful land

— Métis land. He drank in the fresh evening air and glanced over at Pierre, but he was already invisible in the blackness.

Suddenly another black form blocked out the stars. What was it? A heavy body landed on top of him, a hand covered his mouth, stifling his scream, and the cold point of a knife pricked under his chin.

Luc lay still. This man holding the knife had but to twitch and he was finished. He'd left his gun at the top of the ravine, and Pierre couldn't have heard the silent intruder. Luc thought of his mother saying her beads and the words came back, running through his mind of their own accord.

"Hail, Mary, full of grace, the Lord is with thee, Blessed art thou among women. And blessed is the fruit of thy womb, Jesus. Holy Mary Mother of God, pray for us sinners, now and at the hour of our death."

Was this the hour of his death? At least he would die with a prayer on his lips. The thought held no comfort for him. Then his captor laughed, a deep gravel-throated chuckle. Luc stared into the face only inches from him and recognized it with a flood of relief. Gilbert Breland!

"Pierre Gladieu," whispered Breland. "Come here and rescue your partner!" He let go of Luc and stood up, the faint glimmer of his hunting knife extinguished as he put it back in its sheath.

"Mon Dieu!" gasped Pierre. "You gave me a start. Where did you come from?"

"Scared you, did I?" Breland laughed softly. "Just look at young Goyette here. I've put the fear of the devil in him. I followed you from where you tethered your horses – you did pretty well for two youngsters. Good enough to avoid the soldiers, but not if they were using Indian or Métis men themselves. Now listen to me," he hissed in a scolding voice. "Never have both men eating at once. One must always lie and watch. And never, never move without your guns."

After they recovered from their fright they told Gilbert of their instructions from Gabriel Dumont. He seemed worried about leaving two "infants", as he called them, to do the scouting. But he did have many things to tell Gabriel about the soldiers and he thought they would be safe if they were careful. He drilled Luc one more time on his instructions and then led him farther down the coulee where it bent close to the main trail.

Gilbert watched for a few seconds. There was no movement. He took Luc's gun and pushed him up over the edge of the ravine.

"Good luck!"

Luc crouched low and ran swiftly to the path. He could just make out the twin ruts leading to the winking fires of the soldiers' camp. What if he made a mistake? What would these soldiers do to him? NO! Forget all that, be bold! He had to concentrate on the job. Taking a big gulp of the cool night air he stepped off toward the fires.

His nervous energy seemed to put wings on his feet and he reached the camp in no time. A large fire was burning close to the trail and standing beside it were two armed soldiers in dark uniforms. They were so close to the fire that its light would surely blind them. Luc knew that they had no hope of seeing into the darkness. He suddenly felt confident. It would be easy to slip past these sentries unseen. They knew nothing about keeping watch at night. But he remembered Gabriel's orders and resisted the temptation to sneak around them.

"Halt!" the harsh command barked from the darkness behind him. Luc nearly jumped out of his skin; his confidence evaporated. A tall, lean man slowly approached him from the side of the trail. He carried what looked like a Winchester repeating rifle, and had it levelled at Luc's stomach.

Luc's face burned with embarrassment, caught out twice in one night. Some scout he turned out to be. Good thing he hadn't been trying to creep into the camp with his gun! The man, who sported a buckskin jacket and a large slouch hat, motioned for Luc to move on toward the fire.

The two soldiers at the fire didn't see them approach until they actually stepped into the light cast by the flames. Then both men shouted in surprise and whipped their guns to their shoulders.

"Put those things down before you hurt somebody," commanded the slouch hat. "This boy could have walked right past you whistling 'God Save the Queen' and you wouldn't have been a bit the wiser. Now one of you go and call out the guard commander."

* * *

"Captain of the Guard! You there, boy! Where's Captain Lashbrooke?"

Tom dumped his armload of wood near the fire and squatted beside Paddy who was boiling water for coffee. "He's in his tent, two down that way. What's up?"

The soldier, a picket from F Company, shouted over his shoulder as he ran to the Captain's tent. "The Scouts caught an intruder!"

"Coffee can wait, Boyo, this we've got to see." Paddy lifted the pot off the fire and they tied their mugs back onto their belts. They followed the soldier and Captain Lashbrooke down the row of tents out to the picket fire on the main trail.

"It's one of Boulton's men alright," Flaherty pointed to the tall scout. "But where's the intruder?" Tom saw an unarmed boy but no enemy.

"Alright, what's the fuss about? Where's the intruder?" The Captain snapped impatiently. The slouch hat nodded at the civilian.

"You're not serious, man! Boulton's famous Scouts call out the Guard Captain to arrest an unarmed child?"

The scout tapped the boy with the muzzle of his rifle. "Beg pardon sir, but look at the sash and those moccasins. This boy's half-breed sure enough. And what's he doing out alone at this time of night?"

Tom studied the captive. He wore a coarse wool coat and baggy corduroy trousers, but he did have a bright red fringed sash tied round his waist and nicely beaded leggings and moccasins. The face was hidden by shadow, but the scout was right. This one dressed just like the Scotch-Cree freighters his Uncle worked with back home.

"Qu' est-ce que vous appellez vous?" barked Lashbrooke.

"Luc Goyette, Monsieur. I speak English."

"Are you half-breed?"

"I am Métis." Tom recognized a hint of defiance in the voice.

"What? Mustee? What's that?"

"French, sir," the scout interrupted. "Means mixed blood."

"What are you doing here? Where's your home? It's late for a stroll isn't it?" The Captain circled around the boy rapping out the questions. Tom thought about *his* first interview with Lashbrooke.

"I work at the MacIntosh farm, just north a bit." He pointed back up the trail. "And I've come to visit my Uncle Jerome Henry. He drives wagons for you."

Captain Lashbrooke drew the scout aside, near to Tom and Paddy.

"Well? I think we're wasting our time. He's a yokel, no point in interrogating him."

The scout shrugged his shoulders and spat casually. "Might be the best thing to let him go. But let's see if he really does have an Uncle. Then me and my partner can get in position out yonder and follow him when he leaves camp. If he's up to mischief we'll find out." He tapped the stock of his Winchester.

Tom shivered. Everybody in camp knew about Boulton's Scouts. Surveyors, cowboys, traders. They were a tough bunch; the 90th gave them a wide berth, although they wouldn't admit it. That boy would never escape Boulton's men.

"Alright, I'll send Flaherty to escort the boy to the teamsters' lines. After they meet the uncle he can bring him back here. That should take about twenty minutes; is that enough time?"

"Should do, sir." The scout hefted his rifle and disappeared into the dark trees beyond the fire.

"Private Flaherty, did you get that?"

"Yes sir."

"Then fetch your gun and watch this boy. Twenty minutes mind you."

* * *

Luc had only met Henry once before. He had to be sure they did not arouse suspicion. The soldier stuck his head into a tent.

"Here's your nephew come to visit you, Henry."

Jerome Henry came out of the tent, but he didn't recognize Luc. Before he could say anything that would give them away, Luc blurted out, "Hello Uncle Jerome, I bring you a message from Antoine de Padoue."

The man looked confused, "What did you say?"

"It's me, Luc, I've come to see you from Antoine de Padoue!"

Henry smiled, "Ah yes, of course, my boy! It's been a long time. How is Antoine, anyway?"

The soldier seemed satisfied that everything was alright and went to warm himself at one of the nearby fires. Luc explained his mission and told what had happened with the sentries. The teamster was concerned.

"The man with the Winchester repeater, he's got to be one of Boulton's men. They're all old hands, westerners, you won't pull any fast ones on them. We'll have to be very careful when you leave. They'll probably let you go easy enough, then put that one on your tail to follow you. If you lead them back to Breland the game is up for all of us. They'll take you three as prisoners and hang me for a spy."

Hanging. Prisoners. The words hit Luc hard. This was no game, nor was it like hunting. It was deadly serious. Any mistakes now could cost Jerome Henry his life! Luc was at a loss. How could he return to Pierre and Gilbert with the message and at the same time avoid the scout? Henry saw the worried look on Luc's face and laughed aloud.

"Cheer up, Owasis. It'll take a better man than a Boulton Scout to put a rope around Jerome Henry's neck. I have a few tricks up my sleeve too. Look, your guard is more interested in keeping warm than watching over you."

The soldier had his back to them as he hovered near a fire a few feet away. They went to Jerome's tent where he rummaged through his bedroll and produced two scraps of paper. One was a map of the camp at Clark's Crossing and the other was covered with cramped, scratchy handwriting.

Jerome rolled them up in a piece of soft buckskin and fitted the small leather package into Luc's moccasin under the laces that wrapped around his ankle. They then left the tent to sit near one of the campfires. They talked quietly while they sipped cups of hot, bitter tea. Jerome outlined his plan to Luc and together they went over it several times, just as Gabriel Dumont had done back at the store in Batoche.

"Hey you, time to go!" shouted the soldier from the other fire. "I'm not waiting up all night for you."

Luc shook Henry's hand, then hurried off with the soldier. The Captain was still at the big watch fire when they got back, but there was no sign of the scout. Was he gone or was he waiting out there in the dark? Just as Jerome said, there was no problem leaving the camp. They didn't search him or even ask any questions. In fact, the short officer showed no interest at all, which was odd. If he wasn't interested, why wait at the sentry fire?

Luc struck off at a good pace following the trail and was soon enveloped in the darkness. Gradually his eyes adjusted to the black night so that he could distinguish the horizon and the darker patches of poplar bluffs that dotted the prairie. He walked as fast as he could, passing the coulee and on for about another half a mile. Then he stopped suddenly and listened.

Nothing disturbed the quiet night sounds. If the scout was following, he would be moving fast, to keep up. Surely there would be some noise. On the other hand he hadn't heard Breland earlier; why should he hear the scout now? He listened again, holding his breath. Nothing. He resumed his walk but more slowly.

This was also part of Jerome Henry's plan. Any observer would now think that Luc was relaxed, not suspicious, and might himself become a bit careless. Luc walked for another half hour. The trail led into a large mass of trees that stood black in the pale moonlight. The blot of gloomy forest looked forbidding but Luc knew this was his chance. The thick brush closed in around him on all sides so that he could not even see the path or his feet below him.

Remembering Jerome's instructions, he darted forward in a short run then stopped, listened, heard nothing and lay down. At ground level it was so dark he could not see his hand in front of his face. The total blackness was terrifying and he almost leaped back to his feet. But it was protection, so he forced himself to stay down.

Moving like a cat he cautiously began to inch to the left. Soon he felt long grass and the sharp barb of a rosebush that told him he was off the trail. The wild rose pricked his nose, yet he couldn't see it. He found himself staring so hard that his eyes ached but it was hopeless — he was blind. He closed his eyes and instantly felt more comfortable. Keeping his belly on the ground and feeling with his hands and feet he slid quietly into the trees.

He remembered watching a fox run through a poplar bluff once. The little animal had seemed to float over the undergrowth and flow through the trees like water around a rock. Its grace and skill had stuck in his mind. Now he tried to think like the fox. When he felt a tree he eased his body around it. Logs and dry branches he carefully crawled past, never putting any weight on them. His heart was hammering, thumping in his ears. The rhythm seemed to say, *hur-ry, hur-ry, hur-ry.*

He began to feel in the damp earth for a hiding place. A small fallen tree trunk blocked his way. He carefully lifted himself to his hands and knees, passed over the trunk then flattened on the other side.

He lay still now. There would be no better cover for him. His breath came in short gasps. The thought of that scout, deadly and unseen, following him in the dark, was chilling. He gripped the damp leaves that carpeted the ground, and their rotting sweet aroma filled his nose. But the fear of the scout would not go away. The darkness closed in like a shroud of evil and he was afraid to re-open his eyes. Puffing for air, he felt panic rising like a sick lump in his throat. Searching inside his sash he pulled out the small leather patch with the horse embroidered on it.

Just the touch of Marie's gift calmed him. He squeezed it tightly in his fist and her face appeared like magic. She smiled, and the panic faded. He opened his eyes and blinked in surprise. He could actually make out the dark shape of the tree trunk in front of his face. Looking up, a few stars and the sliver of moon hovered above the trees. All he could do now was wait. Anyone following him would have to be along soon.

Time was like the dark. He could not penetrate it. Had he been lying here a minute or an hour? The cold from the damp ground was already creeping through his clothes into his body. Surely it was safe now to go. He remembered his father's words: *let your enemy do the moving; let him make the mistakes.* Good advice, but what if the scout wasn't following? He concentrated on the night sounds. Nothing moved. He decided to count to two hundred slowly. If nothing happened by then it would be safe to go. He longed to be back with Pierre and Breland.

Luc was still counting when he heard the voice.

"It's darker than the devil's hat band in here," it whispered.

"Shhhhh — quiet you fool."

They were only a few feet away. Luc impulsively peeked over the log and saw the outlines of two slouch hats against the sky. They blacked out the stars just like Gilbert had done. He could even see a glimmer of moonlight reflected from the barrel of a gun. They faced forward, looking down the trail, not in Luc's direction. He lowered his head and buried his face in his hands, hardly breathing.

"Hail Mary, full of grace, the Lord is with thee, blessed art thou among women," the words flew through his head again, of their own will.

He mentally screamed at the men to move on but they stood still listening, for him. His leg twitched involuntarily — it wanted to run. Luc was certain they would see him any second, his body tensed, waiting for them to strike. He gripped the small embroidered horse and forced himself to lie like a stone. Visions of Jerome Henry on a hangman's noose, Gilbert Breland's knife and the wicked repeating rifle flashed through his mind. He shut them out and concentrated on the men standing only a few yards away.

Now came their footsteps, clear and soft. They wore boots. Luc was surprised at himself; he could tell the sound of a boot as different from a moccasin. Their footfalls picked up speed and moved on down the trail, away from him. Soon it was quiet again. Luc no longer felt the cold; sweat streamed down his neck and under his arms.

A minute later he was out on the trail heading back to the Crossing. Jerome said if he could give them the slip and then double back quickly they would never catch up to him again. Jerome was right. Luc broke into a trot, then a full run. He was a deer; the faster he ran the stronger he felt. Cool night air whipped past his face, he gulped in huge mouthfuls. Each pounding step seemed to drive a bit more of the fear away. He glanced behind, the terror-filled woods were no longer in sight. He was giddy and began to giggle. The sound of his voice made him laugh out loud. He had done it; he was free!

Finding Pierre and Gilbert was easy. They had watched him pass by with the two scouts on his tail and in turn had followed the scouts. Luc got his fourth surprise of the night when he ran smack into them.

Back in the safety of the coulee Luc turned over Jerome's messages. "Well done young Luc!" Gilbert said. "You were very clever, and as brave as any man I know."

Luc's face flushed. "It was Jerome's plan. I just did what he told me."

Gilbert tucked the messages into his blouse. "Telling and doing are two different things Luc. You have *soketahawin*." He gave them a final warning to be careful, then disappeared down the gully.

Pierre stood watch while Luc lay down. He rolled up in his blankets, but he was still trembling with excitement. He couldn't possibly fall asleep.

"Wake up!"

Pierre's voice jolted him. It was light, he had slept the whole night! "They're moving out Luc. We must get the message back to Batoche."

Luc scrambled to his feet and followed Pierre to the top of the coulee. Sure enough the tents were all down and the soldiers were loading their wagons. "They started early, before daybreak, to knock down their tents. I wasn't sure what they were up to but now I am." A horn tooted in the distance, the same pretty tune over and over. The soldiers ran obediently into line.

"Look over there."

Luc followed Pierre's pointing finger and saw a dozen riders moving up the main trail toward them. The same trail he had followed last night with the scouts behind him. It looked so innocent in the daylight; last night was like an old nightmare. These men didn't ride like soldiers. They were loosely spread out, only one of them wore a uniform; a scarlet jacket with a white helmet. The others all wore long dusters or duffel coats and big slouch hats. They rode as well as Métis and carried Winchester repeaters across their fronts.

"Boulton's Scouts" Luc said. "That's trouble. It was them following me last night. Jerome says they're good."

"Right! They'll be scouting ahead of the main body. Looks like they'll follow the trail up the river. Get back to Gabriel quick as you can, I'll stay here and keep an eye on them."

Luc started to protest but Pierre cut him short. "NO! you did well last night, Luc. It's my turn to take the risk. Get back to the horses now and move fast or those 'Boultons' will get ahead of you on the trail."

He needed no more urging. He wished Pierre luck, grabbed his rifle, and scrambled down the coulee, eager to put the Crossing and its memories behind him.

* * *

Tom could feel the excitement; this was it. Captain Lashbrooke had said they were marching north on Batoche to confront the enemy in battle. Even his bugle was lively this morning. It leaped in his hands, singing the assembly call. G Company men threw the last pieces of baggage on the wagons and ran to form ranks.

"Confront the enemy." The Captain's words echoed in his head. Was that boy last night really the enemy or just a farmer? He sure knew how to move fast at night. Boulton's men had lost him and never caught up. He must have run all the way home. Paddy said the boy's uncle was "just a Frenchman mule skinner. No more a spy than me grandmother."

5. The First Shots

The men were formed up in ranks, like a long picket fence waiting in the predawn gloom, for the command to begin the march. Tom's uncle was standing nearby talking to Captain Lashbrooke.

"We're a small enough force as it is, Sir. We shouldn't split up. With half our men on the other side of the river, the rebels can concentrate their whole army against us and attack before the other troops could return to help."

The bottom of the river valley was still dark, but the high banks on the far side were just visible. Tom strained his eyes for a glimpse of the soldiers over there. What was that thin white line on the horizon? The 10th Royal Grenadiers from Toronto wore scarlet uniforms with white belts and webbing. Was it them? General Middleton had ordered the 10th Royals and Winnipeg

Artillery to shift to the north shore. It had taken three days to ferry the men and their supplies across.

"This is campaign strategy Kerslake," snapped the Captain. "And it's best left to the General. He's afraid the half-breeds won't fight and he wants to be sure to catch them no matter which side of the river they're on. We have more than enough men to handle a few rebels."

"Aye, if there *are* only a few rebels." Jim pulled a soft cloth from his haversack and wiped a thin film of dew from his rifle barrel. "Custer was afraid the Sioux would escape him without a fight remember? Then he ran into two thousand warriors and was wiped out."

"We shan't be so foolish as they were," snorted Lashbrooke. "Besides, they didn't have the Winnipeg Rifles. With all our training of the last few weeks, we're ready for anything, I'll wager."

Jim put the cloth away and slung his rifle over his shoulder.

"As you say sir!" He saluted and went to his place at the end of the company. Uncle Jim still wasn't happy with their drill and discipline, even though he had worked them hard and they were the best company in the regiment. Presently the order to march was given and all thoughts of strategy and massacre vanished as the column moved off.

The sun peeped over the horizon. The long column of soldiers marched directly into the sunrise. The trek from Qu'Appelle to Clark's Crossing had hardened the men. They moved along at a steady pace, in good spirits.

The snow and cold seemed to have been left behind on the desolate prairie. The Saskatchewan River country was dotted with bluffs of poplar and the trail followed mostly high, firm ground near the River. As the sun climbed into the pastel sky the column halted for a break and most of the men removed their heavy greatcoats.

Tom was happy to be on the trail again, and the marching wasn't much of a chore at all. The fresh air and bright sun brought out the best in the soldiers and they began singing their favorite songs. Tom joined in, at the top of his voice, at least when he knew the words. Some of the songs contained what his father called saloon language and Violet certainly would not have approved of them. As the morning passed he found himself thinking about Father and his reluctance to move away from Winnipeg to homestead in this territory.

Uncle Jim had said the opportunities were as boundless as the land itself. Tom now understood what his uncle had been talking about. The South branch of the mighty Saskatchewan River cut a deep gorge in the prairie to their left. The broad highway of water twisted and curved off to the very edge of the earth where it joined the sky. The Batoche trail was a dark brown ribbon. It led them through gentle hills wrapped here and there with scarves of trees. It was a wild and free country. The sight of it filled Tom with an urge to run to the top of the tall river bank and shout, just for the fun of it.

The land was here for the taking. The first ones would have their pick, and Tom agreed with his uncle that they could be some of the first ones. Images of the Kerslakes as wealthy landowners popped into his imagination. He hardly noticed the time go by and before he knew it they were stopping for lunch.

The morning march had gone so well that they were allowed an extra long break for their meal. When the time came to resume the march, Captain Lashbrooke motioned for Tom to blow the assembly call. The Sergeant Major insisted that he move smartly whenever on the Captain's orders, so Tom ran to his position.

He passed close to Corporal Snell and his men, lounging on the ground smoking their pipes. Tom had been careful to stay out of Snell's way since Qu'-Appelle. As he jogged past them, Snell's leg shot out and hooked Tom's ankle, tumbling him in the dirt.

Tom leaped to his feet and furiously looked toward the Captain. Surely Snell would be in trouble now!

"Clumsy boy! That tin horn too much for you to carry, Kerslake?" Snell's cronies as usual laughed at his lame joke. "Too bad the Sergeant Major didn't see that his pet had a fall, eh boys?"

It was true, Snell would never bully him in view of either the Captain or his uncle.

"Come on, Kerslake! Leave off the bugle for a minute, let us men finish our tobacco. No other company is falling in yet," taunted Snell. "Besides, old

General Big Belly will never find us a rebel to fight, so why the hurry?"

Tom controlled his anger with an effort. But he noticed Snell got the men moving very quickly once assembly call started. It was always the same, he knew Snell was a bully but to the officers and even his uncle, Snell seemed to be an efficient NCO. They were soon formed up and stood waiting for the order to march.

"What now? Hurry up and wait!" Patrick Flaherty thumped his rifle butt on the ground and leaned on the muzzle. "What an army!"

"Here they come. Steady up men!" Captain Lashbrooke strode to the front of the company.

General Middleton cantered up from the rear of the column. Two of Boulton's men and the aides followed him, their horses were blowing hard. They reined in opposite G Company. The General's leggings and boots were mud spattered but the blue tunic was spotless.

"I am pleased with our march of this morning." He shook off one glove and straightened the tips of his moustache. "It showed discipline and energy; the very things we will need to put an end to this insurrection. I have just heard from our comrades on the other side of the river that they had a brush with an enemy scouting party early this morning."

A buzz of excitement went through the ranks of soldiers. Everyone was talking at once.

"At last some action!" "Worse luck we missed out!"
"Hope we get a chance!"

Captain Lashbrooke fairly danced with excitement
and clapped Tom on the shoulder. "They knew better
than to tackle the Winnipeg Rifles, eh my boy? Never
mind, we'll get a crack at them!"

The general held up his hand. "The enemy turned
tail after firing a few shots; I am certain they will think
twice about making a full scale attack. However, I
am determined to bring them to heel. Should such an
opportunity present itself to this column, I will expect
every man to exert himself to the utmost to run the
rebel to ground before he can escape. Once we catch
the enemy we will surely thrash him!"

The men roared their approval, and to Tom's amaze-
ment, it was Snell's voice that rang out above the others.
"Three cheers for General Middleton!" Each successive
cheer was more enthusiastic than the last and several
men threw their hats into the air. Only minutes earlier
Snell had been complaining loud and long. Now he was
cheering "Old General Big Belly"! Tom didn't know
what to think about Snell.

They marched only eight more miles before camping that night at a small farm. The house and barn had
been ransacked by the rebels; but otherwise there was no
sight of the enemy. Perhaps they would just run away
without a fight. Tom contented himself with watching
the spectacular sunset. The fiery red and orange bursts
of light from the western horizon blazed like a gigantic

fire. Before he turned in, Tom noticed that his uncle had doubled the sentries and was going round checking each one.

* * *

Luc rode toward the same blazing sunset, leaving Batoche behind. He couldn't decide whether he was more hungry than tired or more tired than hungry. Most of the men riding with him had at least had a good night's sleep and a decent meal before leaving the village. After avoiding Boulton's scouts, he had ridden hard from the Crossing back home to bring the warning that the troops were coming. The Métis army had mounted up at once to go ambush the soldiers. Luc could have stayed behind in Batoche. Gabriel Dumont himself had praised him for his good work and offered to let him stay back. Luc would have gladly gone to bed and slept for a week right then but Larouche had interfered.

"Go home boy, and send your father out to fight — if he's not afraid." How could he ignore that?

The raid was going to be the biggest attack yet mounted by the Métis army. Louis Riel rode one of Gabriel's horses at the head of the army. Dumont carried Le Petit and a belt full of cartridges while Riel balanced a large wooden cross on his shoulder. Such a strange pair. Luc wished that Riel had stayed back; Gabriel Dumont would take care of them. What did Riel know about ambushes?

"Arrêtez! Arrêtez ici." Dumont's command echoed back down the trail. Luc slid from his pony and joined the others where they gathered around Riel. He stood the large cross on the ground and pulled out a set of rosary beads. Gabriel kneeled and crossed himself; Luc did the same.

"Hail Mary full of grace." Luc said the prayer automatically. How different it had been when the words had flashed through his mind last night. The thought of those dark woods and the moonlight glinting off of the Winchester sent a shiver down his neck. But there were two hundred Métis men kneeling beside him now. And standing back with the horses were Cree and even Dakota men.

"Kipa!" They were anxious to go on, they had no patience for Christian prayers.

Not all of the men were tough old hunters and warriors. Many of them didn't even have a rifle as good as Luc's. Before the end of the last prayer, Henri Rochelot stood and went to get his horse. Several others followed him back up the trail toward home.

"Vendu! Come back cowards!" Larouche's harsh insult chased after them.

"No!" It was Riel. He picked up his cross. "Their faith is weak. Pity them, but do not ridicule them." Another five men slipped away into the darkness at the next prayer stop.

They were approaching Roger Goulet's farm and word was passed back from the front that they would stop for supper. Food at last! Even though he hadn't eaten all day, Luc was careful to find water and feed for his horse. It was nearly exhausted and Luc knew how important horses were to a war party. He told himself that when they moved on he would have to walk at the horse's side. Where would he find the strength for that!

He hurried off to where the other men were cooking an ox *en apola*. Luc was not sure if Goulet had given them permission to slaughter his ox but as Gabriel said, this was war and the men needed to eat. The meat was tough and underdone but Luc gorged himself. He then curled up by the warmth of the fire to try to get some rest. Weariness pressed his eyelids shut. The tensions of the day eased slowly from his aching body as he drifted off to sleep.

A sudden shout and the sound of galloping horses disrupted the night. Luc jumped up as two riders reined in their horses calling for Riel and Dumont. The men crowded around. Luc, being the smallest and youngest one there, was able to squirm his way to the front of the crowd where Riel and Dumont were talking to the two men. They had come from Batoche. Their horses were lathered and blown. The men themselves panted for breath; they had ridden hard.

"The Police are coming! Two hundred at least from the south! We need more men to defend Batoche, tonight!" one of them gasped.

"I knew it was a mistake to leave the village!" Maxime Legault bellowed. "We must go back now!"

"My wife and children!" Voices, on the verge of panic, babbled all at once. "God help us — there's only fifty men in Batoche!" "Can we make it back in time. . . ."

Luc thought of his own family. His father had been loyal but would the police know that? Not likely. They take revenge for Duck Lake, destroying every Métis farm in the area, and *their* farm was right on the main trail. Luc gripped the stock of his rifle, he must get back to them, and now!

Some of the men were running to get their horses, while others pressed the two riders for more details. Suddenly a voice roared out above all the others.

"STOP, all of you listen to me!" It was Gabriel Dumont. The men went quiet. Dumont strode angrily to one of the cooking fires so that all could see him. He thrust his rifle into the air and shouted again. "Listen to me! I am the Captain, I will give the order to go back or not."

The men formed a half circle around Dumont. His short powerful body was a black outline against the fire. He scratched savagely at the long scar on the top of his head. Gabriel glared at the quiet group of men for a moment, then spoke in a harsh, critical voice.

"This is a mistake. There were no police moving from either Qu'Appelle or Prince Albert this morning. I have men watching the trails. I tell you that NO policeman could be near Batoche tonight! We do NOT turn back."

Luc could see the dark eyes flashing in the flickering light of the fire; they were full of anger and danger. It would be a brave man who defied Gabriel Dumont this night. Only one man could challenge him. Louis Riel, clutching his cross, stepped into the firelight beside Dumont.

"Are you certain no policeman got past your scouts?" He motioned to one of the riders. "Moise Carriere, come here. Who brought the news of the police?"

Carriere was afraid of Dumont, but he had to answer the question; Riel was the master. "A Cree named Meitatinas saw them on the Qu'Appelle trail. They were coming with great speed," Carriere answered quietly. Dumont snorted with disbelief, but Riel thanked Moise for the news anyway.

Riel bent down to rest the cross on the ground but it slipped. The tip of the crucifix flopped in the grass at Luc's feet. Instinctively Luc knelt, and lifted it. An ice cold hand gripped his wrist; he looked up and found himself face to face with Louis Riel. His eyes were calm, flat, none of the fire from the Novena. Not crazy — not tonight anyway. Luc released the cross and pushed back into the crowd. Riel turned to face Dumont.

"If the police got past your scouts and were moving fast, what then? If Meitatinas is right, we may come back to find our families in chains, and our beloved Batoche occupied by the English. Can we take the risk?"

Dumont lost the struggle to control his temper. He took an angry step towards Riel. "Your beloved Batoche! Always it is Batoche! If we do not hit the soldiers now and again and again, then they WILL capture your Batoche. Just like Duck Lake, we could have killed many but you had not the stomach for it. Now you will protect these soldiers the same way!"

It made Luc sick to see the leaders bickering. How could they fight the soldiers if they fought each other? Yet Riel did not get angry; he spoke again in an even voice.

"I am sorry, my ways are not the old ways of the hunt. But let me take just fifty men back to Batoche in case the police do come. Then we can hold them until you have raided the soldiers and return."

Dumont went quiet, and thought for a moment. "Alright, but I choose those who will return. All men line up here, quickly."

Gilbert Breland, standing beside Luc, chuckled to himself. "The old fox! He'll send the weak and faint-hearted back to Batoche. They'll do him no good in the fight anyway and this way he can be free of Riel's conscience, too."

Gilbert was right. The fifty men selected had poor weapons or had shown little enthusiasm for the raid anyway. Luc thought for sure that being a boy, he would be picked to go back. But Dumont just nodded when he saw Luc and passed on down the line.

The fifty men, led by Riel, soon disappeared into the night. Luc's heart went with them and he prayed quietly that his family would be kept safe. He found himself thinking of Marie Larouche and said a special prayer for her as well, touching his sash where the small embroidered horse was hidden.

Gabriel Dumont, his anger gone, got them organized and back on the trail. Luc walked beside his horse in the darkness, holding the stirrup strap for support. They passed the Tourond farm and crossed the deep coulee there. Luc felt he knew every foot of the trail, even in the dark, and yawned as he plodded along.

Not long after leaving Tourond's Coulee, Gabriel's voice broke the silence. "Everyone get off the trail, HURRY! And be quiet."

Luc's pulse quickened. He led the pony away from the trail. The sound of a single horse pounding at top speed approached them. Who would be foolhardy enough to gallop in the dark? Dumont's voice rang out, "STOP or I'll fire!"

The lone rider reined in hard and Pierre's voice answered, "It's me — Gladieu. Don't shoot!"

"What news, Pierre?" demanded Gabriel.

"They're about six miles away. I left them when they were stopping to make camp."

"Are they camping on the trail?" Dumont snapped.

"Yes, I think so."

"Can you lead us to them?"

"Of course!" Luc could hear the pride in Pierre's voice. "I can take you right to the General's tent, if you like!"

"Good lad, Pierre," chuckled Gabriel. "Mount up *mes amis*, we'll have to ride hard if we're going to give these Englishmen a midnight party!"

Several of the men whooped. Thankful though he was to be back in the saddle, Luc hoped his pony could stand the pace as they moved off into the prairie night.

The party never took place. Luc struggled to stay awake as he stood by his horse listening to the leaders talk. The eastern horizon showed a faint rim of light where the false dawn was just beginning to glow. Pierre's face was a smudge in the darkness, but Luc could hear the shame and embarrassment in his voice.

"They must have moved away from the trail. I left them not far from here only hours ago! If they stayed on the trail then I tell you their camp must be nearby."

"I should have stayed to watch them," Breland remarked. He did not mean it as a criticism, but it hurt just the same. Pierre had been leading them around for hours in the darkness. "The boy's reasoning is sound, Gabriel. We must find them soon, that many men can't disappear. I'll go on down the trail to see if I can pick up their tracks in the daylight."

Gabriel merely grunted, and slapped Breland on the back. Luc watched Gilbert canter away and wondered at the man's toughness. He never seemed to need sleep. Gabriel motioned for the rest of the men to gather in close.

"It's near dawn. Even if we find the soldiers it will be too light to attack them. You will all go back to

Tourond's farm, get something to eat and wait for me
there."

He pointed at the youngest of his brothers. "Elie,
make sure the men stay off the trail and out of sight.
We'll still have a surprise for the Englishmen but it will
have to wait. Napoleon Nault, come with me. You and
I will find the enemy camp and see what we can learn
about them." He and Nault rode off after Breland.

Luc couldn't have cared less about the enemy camp.
He only wanted to get some sleep and gladly followed
Elie back to the Tourond farm. By the time they covered
the half dozen miles, the sun was clearing the horizon,
but Luc didn't see it. His chin rested on his chest and he
dozed while the pony followed the other horses.

"You, Dakota men! Stay clear of the trail you!" Elie's
voice jolted him awake.

The Dakota had wandered away from the group and
were heading for the main trail. It was only a hundred
yards to their left. It dipped out of sight into the deep
ravine that cut through the Tourond farm, then rose back
up to pass near the farmhouse which glowed white in
the sunlight on the far side of the coulee.

The Dakota men ignored Elie and rode onto the
trail. Their leader was a powerful man, over six feet tall.
He wore a fur cap that sprouted long narrow pheasant
feathers. Luc didn't know them very well; they came from
White Cap's band and only a few of them spoke good
Cree, but the leader's name was Eagle.

"Hey! Sioux! Get off the trail." Elie tried again.

Eagle made a rude gesture and dismounted. They pulled some of Goulet's ox meat from their bags and began to make breakfast.

"We're hungry. We'll eat now. It doesn't matter, there are no soldiers around anyway."

Just the sight of the cooking fires made Luc's mouth water. The rest of the Métis army crossed the ravine, dismounting in Tourond's farmyard. They found one of Madame Tourond's oxen and soon had it butchered.

Luc's fire was just crackling into life when Gabriel Dumont and Napoleon Nault rode in. Gabriel scowled. He stood talking to Elie, pointing back to the other side of the ravine where the Dakota were cooking on the trail.

Luc and Pierre crouched near their own fire, toasting the ox meat. He dipped his stick closer to the flames and the meat sizzled. It was still half raw; only a few more minutes and he would eat it — raw or not. Then it would be time for a sleep in the Tourond's haystack. It looked as good as a feather bed. Pierre was still glum over his failure to lead them to the soldiers' camp but secretly Luc was happy. Surely they would go home now. Even Dumont had to admit the raid was a failure. Luc could hardly wait to tell the children about his adventures.

At last, the meat was cooked. Luc took a huge bite and chewed with great satisfaction. He had scarcely swallowed when the rapid thumping of hooves sounded in the ravine. Gilbert Breland flew into the farmyard.

"They're here! The soldiers are coming up the trail, less than two miles away! Hundreds of them!"

Gabriel swore loudly and kicked at the ground. The fires were doused, and Luc reluctantly put the remainder of the meat into his bag. Gabriel was shouting orders — bawling at them to move faster. He rushed them all down into the bottom of the ravine where the creek flowed in a lazy bend around a stand of poplars. Most of them tied their horses out of sight in the poplars. He then led the dismounted men to the woods that grew along the side of the trail.

He spoke to them sternly. "Make yourselves invisible. Dig down into the ground. Make sure your rifle covers the trail." He gestured to the point where the trail crossed the shallow brook beyond the trees. "When the soldiers ride down into the ravine, Joseph Delorme will fire the first shot. When you hear his shot, everyone will fire at once. KEEP FIRING until all the soldiers are dead. Any that escape back up onto the prairie will be cut off and dealt with by me. We'll treat them like buffalo in a jumping pound!"

The men cheered. Luc shivered. These were the soldiers he had seen at Clark's Crossing. Boulton's men, not buffalo. Buffalo did not carry Winchester rifles and creep around in the dark. The Métis were positioned only twenty yards away from the trail. It would be very short range, like a buffalo slaughter if the plan worked. If not, then it might be hand-to-hand fighting.

Gabriel placed nearly all the men in the ambush position. Luc and Pierre were among the twenty he chose to ride with him back onto the prairie. They followed the trail two hundred yards toward the approaching soldiers, then turned off and entered a large bluff of poplars. Gabriel made them dismount and push their horses back into the bush. Then they settled down to await the arrival of the enemy.

Luc's mouth was dry, his hands trembled as he carefully poured gunpowder from the flask down the barrel of his rifle. When he took a bit of patch cloth from his shot bag and put it in his mouth, the cloth seemed to suck the last bit of saliva from his tongue. He fumbled in the shot bag for a ball, dropped one, then selected another and wrapped it in the wet patch. This he set on the end of the rifle barrel and snapped it into the muzzle. Taking the long wooden ramrod he heaved on the ball and drove it down the barrel in one smooth stroke to seat it on the powder. He then took out a small brass percussion cap but before he could fit it in place Pierre stopped him.

"Nervous my friend?"

Luc swallowed hard and nodded.

"When the shooting started at Duck Lake, I nearly wet myself," Pierre grinned. "I was so scared I fired one shot, then rammed a ball into my gun with no powder! By the time I got it out, the fighting was nearly all over!"

He took the cap from Luc, carefully fitted it over the nipple, and let the hammer down gently. But his hands were shaking too.

"We must not fire too soon or we will ruin the ambush." He gave the rifle back to Luc. "Now lie down. Take up an aiming point back toward the ravine. Don't fire unless Gabriel shoots first. The main thing is to lie still and quiet so the soldiers do not see us. We only shoot those who escape back up."

Luc found that snuggling into the carpet of leaves and undergrowth calmed him. He looked over to where Pierre lay. "I've never shot at anything more dangerous than a deer, Pierre. What was it like to shoot at the policemen at Duck Lake?"

"When I saw them shoot down Isidore, it was easy to shoot back. I am a warrior; you will be too."

Pierre's eyes hardened and Luc felt uneasy. A thought was nagging him. It buzzed inside his head like a mosquito that won't go away until it bites. Luc glanced away from Pierre and the thought blurted out. "Thou Shall Not Kill."

Pierre was startled. "What?"

"My mother, Pierre. The Ten Commandments, it's a terrible sin to kill another person. What would the priests say? I'm not sure I can be a warrior. What if I'm a coward?" The words poured out in a jumble as confused as his thoughts.

Pierre smiled, his eyes softened. He reached across to place his hand on Luc's shoulder. "You're not a

coward. Very few men would have walked into that
soldier camp the way you did. Besides, the priests also
say the family is sacred, and you're just protecting your
family. If the soldiers went home to their families we
wouldn't have to fight."

"I guess so, but . . ." Luc faltered.

"Look at the Dakota and learn from them, Luc."

Eagle knelt in the bush near the horses. He was
singing quietly to himself and looked very fierce with
the paint on his face, even though some of it had worn
off since last night. He was singing, it seemed, to the
rifle that he held up high above his shoulders. Luc felt
stronger as he listened to the chanting voice. He found
the words running through his head again but this time
they ran in tune with the Indian's chant. "Hail Mary,
full of grace, the Lord is with thee, blessed art thou . . ."

* * *

"Well young Tom, fine weather for a hike,"
Captain Lashbrooke tipped his cap forward so the brim
shaded his eyes.

Tom smiled back and squinted into the bright, rising
sun. They were making good time again this morning,
another day's march should bring them almost to
Batoche itself. The sun was warm on his face. The air
was still a bit frosty but he scarcely noticed as they stepped
along. There were two other companies ahead of G in

the order of march. An artillery horse whinnied, Tom glanced back. The big guns drove side by side, just off the trail behind him. Their long iron snouts bobbed along almost gracefully above the prairie grass.

The trail twisted around some poplar bluffs ahead of them. The little green worm of men that was F Company were just going out of sight past the trees. F were the advance guard today and marched about four hundred yards in front of the main column. Boulton's Scouts and the General rode well beyond F Company, to lead the entire army.

The advance guard's dark green uniforms stood out clearly against the dun-coloured grass and grey, leafless trees. As Tom watched, they suddenly stopped. One of Boulton's men appeared and dashed past them toward the main column. The column halted, and soon the rider's news was passed down the ranks. Fresh campfires had been found on the main trail just ahead, with a lot of pony tracks. They were to wait while the scouts investigated. The Captain called the order to rest and all the men sat or squatted down. Uncle Jim came forward to sit beside the Captain who was just pulling out his pipe and stuffing it with tobacco.

"Ha! Some hunters we are!" Lashbrooke grunted as he held a match to his pipe. "A few campfires and pony tracks, so we stop dead. We should speed up, maybe then we'd catch the rascals."

"The General's no fool, Sir." Jim filled his own pipe. "If he suspects a trap he'll scout it first. Boulton's men know what they're up to."

"Boulton's men!" scoffed Lashbrooke. "A pack of jumpy, undisciplined amateurs. What we need in this situation is a little dash, a little . . . ."

He stopped short. Jim held up his hand for silence, then Tom heard it himself. A sharp popping sound from beyond the trees to their front.

"What the Devil?" Lashbrooke puffed furiously on his pipe.

"Gunfire," Jim said simply. "But it's over now."

"See! What did I say! A few half-breeds scared up by Boulton's clumsy men and now they're gone. Just like back at Clark's crossing when they lost that boy."

They climbed to their feet, listening for further shots and staring at the screen of poplars to their front as though they might see through it if they looked hard enough. The only sound came from one of the artillery horses as it tossed its head and snorted, jingling its harness. Then Tom heard another sharp pop; instinctively, he held his breath. He looked at his uncle. The Sergeant Major stood erect, his head cocked like a hunting dog sniffing for its prey. Suddenly, clear as a flute on the cool morning air came the bubbling song of a meadowlark. Tom breathed out; no matter how many times he heard it, that song always filled him with delight.

The lark sang again. As though that was a signal of some kind; it was followed immediately by two more popping sounds, and then a roar of many guns going off all at once. Tom had never heard such a noise, like hundreds of tiny thunderstorms clapping at the same time. It subsided a bit, then roared again, rolling louder and longer than before.

"What's going on up there?" Captain Lashbrooke nervously tapped the ash from his pipe and tucked it back into his pocket.

"Here's your battle, Sir," Uncle Jim spoke loudly over the guns. "That's a couple of hundred rifles anyway. Haven't heard that sound for twenty years, but you never forget it."

The men started talking all at once, milling around out of place but Jim's harsh command brought them back into line and quieted them. Captain Lashbrooke's head was swivelling and craning like a chicken looking for feed but there was nothing to be seen and no new orders. A red-uniformed rider cleared the tree line and stopped at F Company. Seconds later they were running forward and vanished beyond the poplar bluff.

The same rider spurred on to the main column; it was one of the General's aides. He reined in and spoke loudly but calmly so they could all hear.

"General Middleton's compliments to you, Major Boswell. Would you please take three companies and report to him forward." The aide flicked a salute to

Boswell who nodded in return. "As fast as you can manage, Sir. We've been attacked by a large body of rebels and have taken several casualties already."

The aide might just as well have thrown a lightning bolt at them. Major Boswell leaped onto his horse. "B, C, G Companies, 90th Battalion! Follow me — double quick. Company Commanders, skirmish-drill load!"

Captain Lashbrooke and Jim began bawling orders at the men. At the same time the aide was shouting to the artillery to unlimber their guns and open fire. Horses, gun carriages, and limbers wheeled around among the infantry. Artillerymen were cursing and yelling as they swung the big cannons into place.

Before Tom could realize what was happening, G Company was dodging past the neighing horses, around the cannons, and running along the rough trail as fast as they could go. The Sergeant Major ran beside them, bellowing for the men to check their cartridges and look to their rifles. They had practiced this in skirmishing drill many times, but the words sounded so different, now that it was for real.

Tom's heart was pounding like a hammer in his chest. He felt as if he couldn't get enough air into his lungs even though they had only gone a few yards. One of the men dropped his rifle and stopped to pick it up. Several others crashed into him and they all ended in a heap on the ground. Uncle Jim was on them in a flash, hauling them to their feet with kicks and curses, shoving them roughly back into line.

Tom had never seen his uncle like this. He looked mean, like a dog about to bite. It frightened him and gave him strength at the same time. His uncle would see them through this battle. Many of the men were joking and making silly comments, and Captain Lashbrooke was laughing out loud as though he was giddy. It was not at all how Tom imagined a battle would begin. They ran toward the steady clapping of rifle fire.

* * *

The ambush was ruined. Luc was furious, and terrified. Elie Dumont had spotted one of Boulton's men, not on the trail as expected but walking his horse along the edge of the ravine behind them! Gabriel, Elie and six others had gone to capture the scout. No sooner had the Dumonts left than the first of the mounted soldiers appeared in view on the trail. Luc had shrunk himself down into the brush and prayed for Gabriel to hurry back.

The soldiers had ridden slowly until they were nearly opposite Luc. At that precise moment he heard the pounding of hooves behind him. The lone scout was riding as though the devil was after him; the Dumonts had not captured him, but they were hot on his tail. The scout tried to ride around the trees to warn his comrades when two shots banged out. A chunk of his coat flew into the air but he stayed on the horse. Then several more shots and the scout pitched from his saddle rolling into the very bluff of poplars where Luc was hidden. He had just seen a man shot down before his eyes, but he couldn't believe it.

There was no point in hiding now, the trap was sprung. The mounted soldiers on the trail reined in at the sound of the gunshots and looked directly at the bluff. Luc felt they were staring at him personally. The leader, who wore a red coat and a tall white helmet, stood up in his stirrups and pointed. The rest of the men whipped out their rifles and wheeled off the trail. He recognized them now — more Scouts! They rode straight for Luc's hiding spot.

"Jesus, Mary and Joseph!" Pierre yelped. "It's time to go, COME ON!"

Luc was on his feet and sprinting back through the poplars to their horses. For Pierre, who was half-blood Cree and a non-Catholic, to use a religious curse, struck him as funny. One half of his mind was full of horror, cringing and waiting for the Winchesters to open fire at his exposed back, while the other half was giggling at Pierre, the Cree warrior, calling out Holy Names.

Miraculously they reached the horses, leaped on, and were away out the back of the woods without a shot being fired at them. Luc pressed his face down against the surging neck of his pony. It was warm and smelled familiar, friendly. He stole a glance back at Boulton's men. Most were following at the charge. Several of them had stopped and were bringing their rifles to their shoulders.

"WHAM!" The pony stumbled.

Luc flung both arms around the little mare's neck and gripped his knees in terror. She picked up her footing and raced for the coulee. Only then did he realize that the shot had come from his friends. Dozens of them appeared at the edge of the ravine. Joseph Delorme stood, waving them in. Then the whole line crashed with gunfire; smoke billowed thickly. A horse screamed. Luc ducked his head and peeked under his arm. One of Boulton's horses was down; the rider limp on the grass.

The Métis swarmed like bees at the edge of the coulee now; another long rip of gunfire crackled. Slugs zipped past. Then Luc was in the smoke, blind for a fraction of a second, and plunged over the edge. The pony jerked wildly back on her haunches and braced her front legs as they skidded down the slope. Luc grabbed futilely at one of her ears as he sailed over her head.

He found himself jammed into a thick patch of willow bush. Except for badly scratched hands and face he was alright. The pony was standing at the edge of the creek, trembling violently. He ran to her but she was in better shape than he was, she had at least stayed on her feet.

"Luc! Come on." Pierre scrambled past him up the hill to the firing line. Their comrades were shouting and cheering, some even threw their caps into the air. The gun smoke was dense but through it Luc could see several of Boulton's men crouched over, running back down the trail. Four of them were carrying another man who hung slack from their shoulders. The rest of the Scouts showed up as dark bumps lying on the brown winter grass. The enemy were firing, but for every shot they took, ten were sent back.

Luc was mesmerized by the battle scene. Pierre elbowed him. "Start shooting, Luc! We've got them on the run! Another victory for the Métis!"

Smoke puffed from a Scout's rifle off to the left. Then the man knelt up to work the lever action on the gun. Luc tucked the butt of his rifle into his shoulder, pulled back the hammer, settled the front bead sight onto the kneeling figure and touched the trigger. The rifle bucked hard and coughed a cloud of blue smoke. The smoke disappeared but the man still knelt, fiddling with his rifle. Luc's first shot as a Métis warrior was a clean miss.

6.   The Battle

Luc lay flat at the edge of the ravine, the grass and bushes concealed him completely from the enemy. He took careful aim at one of the scouts to his front and squeezed the trigger. It was impossible to see the fall of his shot. He raised himself up on one knee to get a better view of the soldiers but Pierre pulled down, hard.

"Don't be a fool!" Pierre hissed in his ear. "Remember what your father said, stay under cover."

Luc simply nodded and slid down to reload his rifle. He was quite calm now; lying here in the bright morning sun shooting at the scouts. Boulton's men were partly hidden by small dips in the prairie and they were taking snap shots, but he couldn't hear their bullets over the noise of the Métis rifles. It seemed that they couldn't hit anything anyway. No Métis or Indian man had been hurt but two more scouts had been carried off

already. Was the scout who had followed him from
Clark's Crossing out there?

Most of the Métis had the same type of rifle as Luc.
The shooting seemed to rise and fall like a wind as the
men shot then stopped to reload. It was quieter just now.
Luc was measuring a powder charge when he heard the
sound of men cheering. It was far off but unmistakable.

He scrambled back up the bank and saw a long line
of soldiers in black uniforms coming forward on the run.
They were still about two hundred yards away, beyond
the scouts. There was one soldier out in front waving his
sword and looking back over his shoulder to urge the
others on. Who had ever heard of such a way of fighting?
Those soldiers should have been on their bellies
crawling forward instead of standing in full view
cheering.

The rebel line fell almost silent as they watched the
soldiers come on, the morning sun twinkling and flashing from the leader's sword. It was such an easy target;
Luc instinctively aimed at the officer, adjusting so that
his sight was resting high on the sword to compen-
sate for the longer range. The whole line erupted in rifle
fire; the enemy leader dropped like a sack of rocks and
the other soldiers hesitated.

An officer on horseback rode over to them
shouting and waving his arms. The cheering started up
again and they came forward even faster. In no time they
caught up to the scouts. They flopped down and began
firing.

Luc ducked down to reload but before he could finish, the sound of cheering rose again above the steady cracking of the Métis rifles. Back up at the edge of the ravine he could see another line of soldiers. These ones were dressed in bright red uniforms with white cross-belts, and they too were running forward with an officer out in front waving a sword.

They were even easier targets than the black-coated soldiers; they kept a better line and moved more slowly. They were off to Luc's left and while he waited for them to get closer, the left end of the rebel line began firing faster. First one, then another redcoat went limp and dropped to the ground. These soldiers showed no hesitation but simply stepped over the shot men and continued to advance.

"Ha!" Pierre shouted in his ear. "They're like sheep! None of us would attack so foolishly. Now, Luc, let's knock a few more over."

Luc squinted down his rifle. The nearest men to him were about eighty yards away. He could see their cross-belts like a target "X". He picked out one soldier, pulled back on the trigger, and felt the rifle kick hard against his shoulder. The soldier spun around in a half-circle and dropped to one knee. But instead of falling, he simply stood up and kept marching.

Eventually the redcoats stopped in line with the others. Luc did a rough count. There had to be almost a hundred enemy shooting where minutes ago there had only been a handful of scouts. Maybe their tactics weren't so foolish after all.

Now Luc could easily hear the sound of an Englishman's bullet as it passed overhead, snapping like a dry stick broken over your knee. The soldiers had better rifles than most of the Métis and that evened the odds.

"*Thump.*"

He ducked as a shower of dirt and bits of grass sprayed over Pierre. A bullet had gouged the earth about a foot in front of his friend.

"They're getting too close, *N'Sjyaasis*," shouted Pierre as he slid down the ravine wiping the dirt from his face. "If many more come at us, we may not be able to hold them. Be ready to move back into the woods when Gabriel gives the word."

Luc's ears were ringing from the steady banging of the gunfire. He could see Gabriel way off to the right, firing Le Petit with great concentration, ignoring the bullets flying around him. Gabriel was one of the few men who had a repeating rifle, and what was more, he rarely missed any target he aimed at.

But many of those near Luc were not crawling back up to the prairie. They seemed to hover down where it was safe. Luc was taking a long time to reload himself. The incoming bullets were like a swarm of angry bees above them and he hesitated to lift his head.

Pierre was still full of fight; he seemed to enjoy the danger. "Take courage brothers, keep firing, they haven't hit any of us yet." Then suddenly pointing he shouted,

"LOOK, LOOK, there's bravery for you! Watch the young Dakota!"

One of the Dakota men had actually climbed up out of the ravine, and in full view of the soldiers began to shout and jeer at them. Luc could imagine the hail of bullets which must be flying all around the Indian. But he seemed not to care because he just danced a few steps and laughed, shaking his rifle in the air. Luc cringed, surely any second he would be struck, but the Indian took aim and fired his rifle at the soldiers. Only then did he jump back down into the safety of the ravine. Incredibly, he refused to stay there. He grabbed a loaded rifle from Eagle and climbed straight back out onto the flat open prairie.

"He has powers the soldiers don't understand," Pierre crouched beside Luc. "He challenges their leader to personal combat like a true warrior, so their bullets can't touch him. Wandering Spirit, the war chief from Big Bear's band, is said to have the same mas*kiki*."

Luc's eyes were rivetted to the warrior. Was there really such a thing as magic? His father said no, yet his mother kept Jean's letters as a talisman. She once even called the priests Medicine Men when she was talking to her old uncle on One Arrow's reserve. Father Fourmond just laughed when she confessed it to him.

Still, the Dakota was dancing and shouting insults at the soldiers, and there was no crucifix protecting him. Then he stopped dancing and fired another shot. As the smoke cleared from the end of his rifle he began chanting a song.

Luc could not hear the exact words, but he was enthralled by the sight of the young warrior defiantly challenging his enemy to fight. The high piercing voice floated above the rattle of gunfire, carrying clear as the meadowlark's song on the morning air. Luc's heart kept time to the rhythm of the chant and seemed to pump new blood into his veins.

Then, abruptly, the spell was broken. The chant stopped; the Dakota folded in two and fell back over the edge of the ravine where he rolled a few feet farther down and lay still.

Luc's own heart stopped for a fraction of a second. He willed the Indian to get up and continue his song but he lay quiet, the breeze ruffling the two feathers tied to his gun. Gabriel ran crouched over to the warrior and lifted one of his shoulders, only to let it drop limply. Dumont took the rifle and hurried back to his position.

NO! Such courage — wasted! Luc scrambled back up the ravine and fired again at the long line of soldiers, then dropped back down to reload.

"Another one is gone — Paranteau, I think," called Pierre.

A body was stretched out on the side of the ravine. Eli Dumont bent over him for only a second, then took the man's coat and covered his face with it. It was just a month ago that they had met the Paranteaus at the Novena. Now their son was dead.

Luc heaved on the ramrod, pushing the ball down his rifle, and reached for another percussion cap. A new sound carried above the roar of gunfire. It was high-pitched, and demanding. An English bugle calling more soldiers into the battle. Then came more cheering. He glanced nervously at Pierre. His friend's face was grim as they climbed up the bank once more.

* * *

Running over the rough trail to the line of poplar trees had helped to settle Tom's nerves. He could clearly hear the gunfire and shouts from the men fighting on the far side of the trees. The General, his heavy body surprisingly agile, trotted his horse through the bush to meet them. He conferred with Major Boswell briefly. Then Boswell called the company commanders.

"Wait here with the Sergeant Major." Captain Lashbrooke darted off.

Tom looked down the column of G Company men; most were now quiet, panting from the excitement and the exertion of the run. Uncle Jim walked among them checking their ammunition pouches, talking calmly.

"All right Paddy — tighten your cartridge belt, it looks as loose as Grandpa's longjohns. Remember your dressing lads — don't bunch up. Let's show these rebels what we're made of, eh? No stragglers — no excuses G Company."

Minutes later their Captain came striding back to them and gave the order to march. The other two companies went with Major Boswell off to the left, away from the battle, but G Company followed the general into the woods. The underbrush was thick, and grabbed at Tom's ankles. He seemed to stumble every other step.

"Steady lads," Uncle Jim urged them. "Come on G Company — keep your ranks!"

But it was almost impossible to move through the densely packed saplings and stay in column. As they neared the other side of the bluff, the gunfire rose to a crescendo. Lashbrooke bellowed.

"G Company! At the halt, on the right — Form Line!"

The gunshots and battle noise drowned the command. Lashbrooke roared the command again. Half the company tried to move right but it only ended in confusion. Jim was yelling and pulling men into position but nobody could understand him.

The General rode up to Tom and shouted, "Bugler! Do you know the call to 'form line'?"

Tom fumbled for the mouthpiece in his haversack, fitted it into the trumpet, and began playing the long, full notes that told the company to come into line. The effect was magical. The soldiers began moving to their correct places and in seconds G Company stood in two long parallel lines, facing toward the sounds of battle. The General gave him a smile and a nod; Tom saluted proudly.

As they stood waiting for the order to advance something smacked the tree next to Tom; seconds later a twig above him snapped off and dropped onto his head. He ducked down and pulled the stick out of the crease in his Glengarry hat. Bullets were hitting the trees all around them and the men began to flinch and duck their heads, even though they couldn't see where the firing was coming from.

Middleton pushed his horse through the trees and roared out, "Now lads! No ducking! I'd have lost my head if I had been ducking when this hit!" He held his hat up so all the men could see the bullet hole in the brim. It didn't make sense to Tom. Surely the bullet would have missed him altogether if he had ducked down? But the men laughed and gave the General a cheer.

The General waved his hat and slowly walked his horse out of the poplars and onto the open ground beyond the trees. Captain Lashbrooke went with him attended by Uncle Jim. Tom's place was with the Captain so he tagged along behind them. The General was leaning over the neck of his horse pointing at the edge of a ravine to their front. The firing had subsided. Only an occasional shot banged.

"Right now, Lashbrooke," he said, calm as though they were in camp on the parade square. "Take your company forward and line up to the right of the Infantry Corps over there."

Captain Lashbrooke was nervous; he looked first at
the General, then at the Sergeant Major, then over to
where the General was pointing, then back toward the
men. "I'm sorry, General, but where are the enemy?" he
asked. "I don't see them. Where do you want me to go?
How am I supposed to attack them?" he asked.

Patiently the General pointed again and explained. "They
are at the edge of the ravine, hidden, Man. Of course you
can't see them. I want you to tie in on the Infantry
Corps' right flank so the breeds don't get us in
enfilade fire."

Lashbrooke looked wildly around behind them as
though he expected to see the enemy there now. Tom
was as confused as the Captain. Where was the flank
anyway? What was enfilade fire?

The enemy bullets still occasionally snapped
overhead; Tom felt extremely conspicuous standing out
in the open but he wasn't particularly afraid. He had
envisioned long lines of enemy soldiers and heroic
charges; all this talk of flanks and taking cover was
nothing like the pictures of battle he had seen in books.
He could only see a few of their own men lying in the
dips and folds of the ground in front of them; of the
enemy he saw nothing.

Just when it seemed they would never get themselves organized, Uncle Jim stepped forward and spoke,
facing the Captain but in such a way that he was really
talking to the General.

"I believe the General wants us in the firing line just to the right of the redcoats there. Would you like me to act as company guide, Sir?"

The General cut in before Lashbrooke could answer, "Capital idea, Colour Sergeant! Old soldier are you? Been at this before, I'll wager?"

"Yes, Sir" Uncle Jim nodded, touching the brim of his cap. "Western campaign with Grant and Sherman in '63 and '64."

The General positively beamed. "Couldn't be better! Lashbrooke! Make use of this NCO as a guide! When you get in position I'll expect you to hold firm, Captain." He wheeled his horse to canter away.

Captain Lashbrooke looked very relieved. "Carry on, Sergeant Major!" he called in a high voice.

Uncle Jim saluted, "Very good, sir. I'll bring the company up. May I suggest we go slowly, sir, to keep the men in hand?"

"Of course Sergeant Major. G Company will maintain proper discipline in the attack."

Jim ran back to the poplar bush and soon had the men out of the trees and moving forward. Captain Lashbrooke hurried to the front of the company and drew his sword, Tom stayed by his side. They had only gone a few yards when the sound of the enemy rifle fire picked up.

Small clouds of smoke blossomed here and there at the edge of the ravine. As they advanced farther through the tall grass the battle seemed to lull. The only sounds were the swishing of the men's feet tramping down the grass and the click and clank of water bottles, bayonets and tin cups banging against their legs.

They drew gradually closer to the ravine. Clumps of Infantry Corps soldiers lay on the ground near the coulee, but they weren't shooting. Abruptly the lull was broken as a ragged volley of enemy rifle fire crashed out and the ravine disappeared in a thick bank of smoke.

The air vibrated with the zip of bullets. Captain Lashbrooke spun around with a shriek, but stayed on his feet; his sword flew through the air end over end. A man Tom knew only as "Smitty" ran up from the rank behind and crashed headlong into Tom knocking them both to the ground. As Tom scrambled to his feet, he saw that Smitty was holding both hands to his face, his cap was gone and a thin stream of blood trickled down from his hair. Smitty kept saying, "I'm alright, I'm alright" as he rolled around on the ground.

Half a dozen men crowded around to gawk at Smitty. The evenly spaced ranks began to break up. More rebel bullets cracked close overhead. Tom looked wildly around and saw Captain Lashbrooke stooping to pick his sword up off the ground. Everything seemed to be happening in slow motion. Lashbrooke looked directly at Tom and screamed, "Sound the charge!"

Tom's hand jerked the bugle up and the strident staccato notes leapt from the horn. The Captain waved his sword in the air and bellowed, "Follow me, G Company" as he took off at a dead run.

Smitty was forgotten; the men surged forward in a tight knot behind their leader. Tom, sprinting to catch up to the Captain, saw that they were no longer heading toward the ravine but were running parallel to it. A man tripped and went down beside him with a curse; Tom dodged him and ran on. It was all a mess — confusion. Tom felt fear and panic begin to rise from the pit of his stomach.

A hand descended on his shoulder in an iron grip jolting him backwards. He could hear Jim's voice roaring above the sounds of the battle. "Captain Lashbrooke, Sir!" Jim was on the Captain in a trice and grabbed him roughly, shaking him.

"With your permission, Sir, we'll be better in our position over there." He pointed back to the ravine. "I'll show you; this way, Sir."

Jim physically led the Captain in the right direction and at the same time shouted the men back into place, slowing them down from their pell-mell charge. Tom was astounded how polite his Uncle was in the midst of the pandemonium. Order was gradually restored; Jim stayed up front with the Captain. The men followed, not in perfect ranks, but at least the panic was gone. The enemy rifle fire had died away.

Jim led them forward at a dog trot which soon brought them up to the line of Infantry Corps redcoats. It was quiet again. G Company slowed to a walk and began to straighten its ranks.

"CRRRAAAAK."

A flurry of shots rang out from the ravine, now only yards to the front. Captain Lashbrooke's water bottle exploded spraying over Tom. The heavy smell of alcohol filled his nostrils.

"Mother! Oh my sainted Mother!" someone screeched.

Tom whirled around, recognizing the Irish accent. Patrick Flaherty was squirming on the ground like a caterpillar, wriggling and clawing at his side.

"Get Down, G! Down!" Jim's command drowned Paddy's whimpers.

A terrific roar burst out from every rifle in the army's line to answer the enemy volley. Tom flung himself to the ground and buried his face in the dry grass. Through the tangled stalks he could see a couple of men nearby bringing their rifles to their shoulders, although what they could see to shoot at, he didn't know. Paddy was still moaning and crying. Tom couldn't bring himself to look. The enemy rifles were banging away, their bullets cutting the air overhead. Tom hugged the earth and squeezed his eyes shut trying to block out the gunfire.

Then a new sound rose above all others on the battlefield. It was the sound of cloth tearing, except much louder and it seemed to split the sky. Tom looked up instinctively but saw nothing. A loud bang shook the air and a small dirty grey cloud sprouted above the far side of the ravine. Seconds later another brief rip followed closely by a bang produced a second burst of smoke, this time closer to the edge of the ravine. The enemy rifle fire stopped, and the soldiers' fire slackened to a couple of random shots. Everyone looked up for the next explosion.

"Shellfire!" crowed Uncle Jim. "The artillery are finally in the show." His uncle was walking calmly amongst the G Company men talking to them, correcting their aim, smiling as though it was a Sunday picnic. Not far away Corporal Snell struggled to lift Flaherty's limp body.

"Private Webster!" Snell barked. "On your feet! Help me get this man to the doctor."

They lifted Paddy, one under each arm, and shuffled to the rear. Paddy's head lolled back and he moaned softly. His trousers were ripped open and dragged on the ground. His underwear was soaked red at the belly. An enemy rifle banged and dust exploded at Snell's feet. He ignored the shot.

Tom jerked his eyes away. But the image of Paddy, hanging like a bloody rag doll, would not leave him. He felt sick, and his teeth chattered. Two more rebel shots cracked, a bullet snapped through the grass beside him. He pressed the side of his face hard to the ground.

"Oh God, don't let it be Paddy's time to die! Not Patrick Flaherty."

Even as he prayed, one part of Tom's mind stayed clear and calm. Why hadn't *he* gone to Paddy's side, it asked? Snell might be a bully, but he also had guts.

* * *

Luc knew they were in trouble; the tide of the battle had shifted fully now. The rebel line was close to breaking. Those men still shooting didn't even take proper aim. They just shoved their rifles over the edge of the gully, took a quick sight, pulled the trigger and dropped back down. Every Métis shot brought a half dozen return shots, not very accurate but still dangerous.

Luc was crawling to the top of the bank when "WHOOOSH WHAM" an explosion shook the air. A circle of smoke hung in the sky above the Tourond farmhouse on the other side of the creek. Seconds later came another blast, this time bursting just behind them making the very air vibrate. Luc felt a soft thump of concussion against his chest. What was happening?

A few feet away, Pierre was holding tight to the earth, his eyes shut. There was a strange quiet. No one was firing; they were stunned and surprised. Pierre lifted his face and said one word. "Cannons."

The men began to slowly inch their way back from the edge of the ravine, down toward the small clumps of bush at the bottom near the stream. For several minutes the battlefield was silent. Then two more screeching shells arrived to explode overhead. One of them produced a tight pattern of splashes in the creek. Shrapnel! Luc stared at the bubbling water. If one of those shells burst above him, he would be killed outright; there was no hiding from bullets that came straight down out of the sky. The steep bank seemed the safest place; Luc pressed his body flat to it.

The only sounds came from Gabriel Dumont. Le Petit was busy on the right of the firing line. The man was fearless. He shot, ducked down, moved to a new spot and fired again. The cannons didn't bother him in the least. Then Pierre's voice broke the spell.

"Courage Chasseurs!

Ne craignez pas le tapage;

Du canon de ces Anglais."

He jumped to his feet and ran back to the top of the coulee where he flopped down, took careful aim and fired. The men gradually came to life and followed Pierre's lead. Luc climbed back up the bank and found a depression where the Tourond cattle had made a trail on their way from the pasture down to the creek. It was just wide enough for his body. He found that he could actually crawl out onto the flat prairie and remain concealed in the cattle rut.

Peering through the grass he could see the dark green riflemen to his right and the redcoats to his left. If they all charged at once, could the Métis line hold them? Pierre was right; they would have to escape soon.

A mounted soldier rode up opposite Luc and reined in. He began talking to some of the men on the ground. Luc took careful aim on the bright spot of light where the sun glinted from the man's belt buckle and tightened his grip on the trigger. The gun didn't fire. Luc relaxed his finger. What was wrong with him?

That soldier was one of their leaders. It would be a great feat to down one of their officers. Why had he shied from pulling the trigger? He took careful aim again but still could not bring himself to shoot. It seemed so cold-blooded. When the soldiers had been charging, Luc hadn't thought twice about shooting back but this man seemed so harmless sitting there on his horse, no gun, just chatting.

"Thou shall not kill!" The words buzzed inside his head. His Mother's words. He scolded himself. "Some warrior, Luc Goyette! Afraid to fire his gun!" He thought of Isidore Dumont and Paranteau; nobody had given them a second chance. Gritting his teeth he aimed once more, quickly, and snatched at the trigger, hoping in his heart that he would miss, although a man and horse made a big target at such short range.

The rifle banged and the horse reared wildly back on its haunches. It fell with a scream, kicking up a cloud of dust. The rider was thrown hard. He got slowly to his feet and walked to the rear, limping. Luc wriggled back down the cow rut into the ravine. He didn't like shooting horses but at least his conscience was clear. He had done his duty and the officer was out of the fight.

Pierre was missing. Luc searched the firing line frantically before he spotted his friend near the stream. He was talking to two men who were in the poplar bluff, with the horses. The men mounted and rode clear of the trees — deserters? No, it was Gabriel and Napoleon Nault.

They spurred their animals and rode down the creek. Moments later they emerged onto the main trail and passed through the Tourond farm. What was going on?

"Hey! What's this?" Larouche stood part way down the slope, pointing at the riders. "They're leaving us!"

The men slid down from the prairie and the firing died away.

"They'll be back." Pierre ran up from the creek shouting. The left end of our line broke and ran from the cannon fire. Gabriel has said we are to hold our positions here. He'll bring them back to support us."

"I don't believe it!" Larouche stomped down the hill to confront Pierre. "They've made their escape while we sit like fools protecting their backs. I say we get out now! This young pup," he gestured toward Pierre, "knows nothing. He's been duped."

"The young pup is telling the truth!" It was Joseph Delorme. He stepped out from the trees to the left.

"There are only twenty of us in the woods, the others ran when the cannons started firing. They were caught in the open, no cover. We twenty will hold the left but you must stay in position here until Gabriel returns." He waved his arm and descended to the water. "Come down into the bottom of the coulee and make yourselves shelters. You won't survive up on the prairie. Then when the English come over the top, you can shoot them like rabbits on the crest."

Joseph Delorme was well respected. His instructions made sense. Luc needed no coaxing to leave the dangerous embankment. Bullets were now combing the edge regularly, but at least the big cannons had fallen silent.

Luc followed Pierre down to the edge of the creek. There were trees here to hide behind. The Tourond cattle had made deep grooves along the stream which might shield a man from the cannons if they started up again. They began piling rocks and logs around the ruts, putting the trees between themselves and the enemy. Larouche moved along the shore of the creek cursing the men for fools.

"Stay if you like," he snarled. "This is crazy. Those soldiers have us outnumbered. They'll show no mercy when they attack again. Dumont has deserted us."

He took a kick at the logs Luc was piling up and sent them flying. Pierre sprang like a cat, fists flying, and landed a sharp blow to Larouche's head.

"Gabriel Dumont will never desert us!" he screamed. "You're the coward, Larouche. Go on — get out of here, we don't need you!"

Larouche, although twice the weight of Pierre, was staggered by the sudden attack and backed off.

"You'll regret that, Gladieu," he muttered.

He thrust his rifle into Pierre's face. "I was fighting and hunting long before you two were born — you know nothing! I tell you it's every man for himself now."

He laughed and turned to leave. "You can cover my retreat, children. I'll deal with you later — *if* the Englishmen don't butcher you first."

Luc retrieved the logs and this time wedged them securely between two poplar saplings growing near the cow trail. The rut was a foot deep and ran parallel to the creek which gurgled in the bottom of the ravine only a few feet away. The poplars were quite thick and were interspersed with willows. Pierre hauled some large rocks from the creek bed and planted them along the edge of the rut behind the logs Luc had piled. In a few minutes they had erected a solid barricade facing up the hillside. By lying in the cow trail they had nearly two feet of protection and yet without exposing themselves too much they could still see the crest over which the soldiers would soon appear.

It was very quiet now. There was no shooting, the only sounds were the creek flowing behind them and two comrades working on another shelter nearby. They were actually standing in the water itself and carving a small cave out of the bank.

A lone rider appeared in the Tourond farmyard. It was Larouche.

"Good riddance!" Pierre spat. "I don't blame him for running out. Who would share their rifle pit with Larouche? Nobody trusts him — he can't count one true friend among us."

Luc lay back in the bottom of his trench, worn out. The lack of sleep and food, and the terrors of the battle had left him feeling sick. He took the embroidered horse patch from his sash and squeezed it in his hand. Pierre saw it and grinned.

"Hey! What's a good Catholic like you doing with a Cree talisman?" he teased.

"It's a present from a friend. It feels safe, that's all."

Pierre smirked. "So a friend gave you that. Not many can do such fine needlework; the friend wouldn't be Marie Larouche would it?"

Luc said nothing but his face blushed furiously.

"A hah! I'm right!" laughed Pierre. "She's pretty. You're lucky, but I don't envy Larouche as a father-in-law! Maybe that talisman will protect you from both the Englishmen and her father!"

"It's not a talisman, just a present," Luc retorted.

"A very special present, made by your woman, that keeps you safe," Pierre recited the facts. "I don't know what your Catholic priests say about that, but to the Cree it is powerful and only a fool denies it. The Cree people have lived on this land a long time. Your priests are newcomers, they don't know everything."

Luc didn't reply. He remembered how he had mixed the Catholic "Hail Marys" in with the Dakota war song just before the fighting had started. But Pierre had called on Jesus, Mary and Joseph for protection too. Mixed blood could make things very confusing. Better to take the best from both worlds because it looked like they would need all the help they could get.

These thoughts and his fatigue gradually overcame him. Presently his head lolled back and he slept.

* * *

Tom sat on the warm dry grass, his legs stretched out in front of him. The men of G Company were prone in the firing line about twenty yards away but there was no shooting. It looked as though the enemy had retreated; at any rate they had stopped shooting and about fifty rebels had been seen fleeing past the farmhouse on the far side of the ravine. The artillery had chased them with a couple of long-range shells.

Captain Lashbrooke and his Uncle were discussing the battle while Tom soaked up the sun. He took his mouthpiece from the bugle; it was full of dirt. He must have fallen on it. He dug a small piece of cleaning cloth out of his haversack and began to wipe the plugged opening.

He tried to thread the cloth into the hole but his hands were trembling so badly that he dropped the mouthpiece. He tried again but he couldn't control the shaking. What was wrong with him? Embarrassed that someone might see him quivering like a terrified rabbit, he put the cloth away. Taking a deep breath, he lay back and tried to relax. At least it was over and he had survived his first battle.

Captain Lashbrooke had had some narrow escapes. In addition to the water bottle – rum bottle, rather — shot from his side; his sword scabbard had been hit, his sword had been shot out of his hand, and there was a bullet hole in the skirt of his tunic. Jim had his pipe out and was filling it with tobacco. Tom was surprised to see his uncle trembling so badly that he had to steady the pipe with both hands to get it lit. Jim's eye locked with his.

"Hot work, Tom, my boy." He winked at Tom and blew his match out. Taking a great puff on his pipe, he frowned thoughtfully. "Lucky we only lost two. Smitty should be alright but Flaherty looked serious to me."

"Aye, well we've whipped 'em now. They'll not likely tangle with us again soon." Lashbrooke fingered the hole in his tunic.

"Don't count on that, Sir," Jim replied. "I think we've only begun. There's still rebels down in the bottom of that ravine and I'll wager we'll have the devil of a time to dig 'em out."

Captain Lashbrooke's smug expression vanished.

"You're not serious are you? We've had enough for one day I think."

Jim nodded at the approaching figure of Major Buchan. "I imagine we'll find out right soon, Sir."

Sure enough, Major Buchan arrived with orders for G Company to leave its position and move to the far west end of the ravine, where the artillery and Major Boswell were located. There was going to be an attack and they were going to be part of it. Tom brushed the dirt from his trumpet and began sounding the assembly call.

G Company obediently pulled out of the firing line, and gathered around their bugler.

7.   Face to Face

Luc woke up with a start. His heart was thumping as though he had just run a race. The log on the top of their barricade showed a gaping split, the clean wood shone where the old bark had been torn away. The air reeked with a strange sulphur smell. Pierre lay flat in the bottom of their trench with his hands clasped over his head.

"What's happening? Are they attacking?" Luc craned his neck to see over the wall.

"No attack, Luc. That was the cannon. The shell went off just behind us. Woke you did it?" Pierre sat up grinning. "They've been shooting for about fifteen minutes but mostly at the Tourond farmhouse. Look here, another foot lower and that would have been my head." He stuck his finger in the piece of smashed log. "And you would have slept right through it!"

Luc didn't think it was very funny.

"Don't look so worried," Pierre laughed. "As long as we stay in our snug little home we're quite safe. Come on, get down as low as you can. That way only a direct hit can harm us."

The words "direct hit" weren't very comforting. Luc dropped onto his stomach and, like Pierre, covered his head with his arms. Moments later a terrific bang shook the ground, dust and twigs rained down into the hole and the thud of concussion slapped against his back, knocking the air out of his lungs. A second explosion followed on the heels of the first, taking Luc's breath away before he had gotten it back.

Pierre pulled him up, gasping. "It's alright now for a minute; the shells always come in twos. Then there's a break while they reload."

Luc lifted his face out of the dirt, coughing and spluttering. At least he didn't feel sick, the short nap had cured him, although his body still longed for sleep. Father's rifle lay in the bottom of the trench covered in dirt. Luc picked it up and tucked the lock under his coat to protect it.

The bright sun had given way to low grey clouds. The thunder of the cannons seemed to call for a storm, and now the clouds opened up, pouring out a freezing rain. Two sparrows perched in the branches overhead fluffed out their feathers against the wind and rain. Luc marvelled at the tiny birds. Why would they stay here in the midst of the gunfire? As if in answer to his thoughts,

they chirped loudly to each other and flitted away. Pierre
signalled and Luc stretched out on the damp earth,
holding his breath against the coming explosions.

The rain pelted down through the leafless trees
soaking Luc to the skin. He shivered, huddling in the
bottom of the muddy trench. He'd lost track of how many
times the enemy cannon fire had smashed through the
treetops, buffeting their makeshift shelter. No "Hail
Mary's" came to Luc now, only blank animal dumb-
ness. He didn't think or care about anything. He
stared at Pierre's moccasin, inches from his face. Each
raindrop that hit the soft leather glistened for a second,
then vanished as it soaked in. They were practically lying
on top of each other in the narrow trench.

Then there were no more raindrops. A narrow shaft
of sunlight filtered through the poplars. The clouds were
breaking and scattering. The cannon fire stopped. Perhaps they were through the worst of it. He sat up, looked
at Pierre's grimy face, and was rewarded with a grin.

"Poor shots, eh, my friend?" he laughed. "All that
shooting and they couldn't touch us. Maybe they'll give
up and go home now."

Luc shivered and smiled. Maybe it was over; anyway,
nothing could be worse than those cannons. The high
sharp call of a bugle cut through his thoughts. Another
trumpet, closer, answered the first one and the sound of
men cheering came from the top of the ravine. Luc
shivered again, but not from cold. The soldiers were
coming!

* * *

The artillerymen worked their guns with ruthless precision. Each man had a job and did it with cat-like speed. One would place the powder charge in the barrel, a second would push it in with the long ramrod, then in went the wadding, then the shell, each rammed in succession. The gun captain would take a final check on the sighting, leap clear and yank the lanyard simultaneously. The gun roared and the gunners jumped back to clean, load, aim, and fire again before the smoke from the first shell had disappeared.

At first the guns had concentrated on the distant farmhouse and buildings until they were battered and burning. Then they shifted to fire into the bottom of the ravine where the enemy were supposedly hiding. Tom had still not seen a single Indian or half-breed warrior, even from his new position atop the highest part of the ravine.

He could see where G Company had first attacked farther to the east and the trees where the wagons were circled in a *zareba*. He could also see that even depressing the gun barrels as far as possible, the artillerymen couldn't get their shells to actually hit in the bottom of the ravine. They all exploded up in the tree tops or farther down by the farmhouse.

That was the problem. If the cannons could not reach the enemy in the creek bed, then the infantry would have to put in an assault at close quarters. As far as he was concerned, the artillerymen could go on shooting all day, he didn't know if he could face the hidden rifles again.

Images flashed through his mind. Flaherty writhing on the ground; and bullets smacking into Captain Lashbrooke's sword scabbard and bottle. He looked away from the guns and down the line of G Company men, most of whom huddled quietly in the rain trying to keep warm. Their heavy coats were still loaded on the wagons, so there was no chance of keeping dry.

His uncle and the Captain were standing near the ravine with Major Boswell and two other company commanders. They were pointing and arguing back and forth, planning the new attack. Attack! Tom shuddered and looked back at the guns, trying to concentrate on what they were doing.

"Impressive sight but they don't do much good."

Corporal Snell casually squatted down beside Tom. Tom glanced up but said nothing; the last thing he needed was trouble from Snell. The Corporal as usual didn't seem to be tired or bothered by the miserable, freezing rain. He looked full of energy and puffed happily at his pipe. Snell drew his long sword bayonet from its scabbard and fitted it to the end of the Snider-Enfield rifle with a snap. He waved the wicked, curved blade in front of Tom's face.

"We'll see how those half-breeds like a taste of this beauty eh, Kerslake?" he said with a cruel grin.

Tom pretended not to pay any attention to the weapon but the sight actually gave his stomach a twist. How could Snell seem to like this business so much? Snell took the bayonet off the rifle and put it away.

"Poor Flaherty caught it good. When I took him back to the *zareba* the Doctors just shook their heads. He'll be lucky to see home again," Snell's voice softened.

"He was my friend. I shared a tent with him on the march up here," Tom replied. A stab of conscience nagged him. He couldn't ignore Snell's bravery, however much he loathed the man.

"I also saw you carry him out — thanks."

Snell grunted. "Well, can't just leave a man to die, somebody had to help him."

The corporal dug into his haversack and pulled out some dried meat which he unwrapped, and without a word gave a piece to Tom. Friendship? From Snell, of all people! He hesitated — why should Snell show him any kindness after all the bullying? He stared at the meat; he hadn't eaten since very early in the morning and he was ravenous. He took a large bite. It wasn't even tough old salt pork. It was dried beef and tasted delicious.

"Thank you, Corporal," Tom mumbled through the mouthful. "But why share your food with me?"

"You did alright today, Kerslake. Acted like a proper little soldier. I had figured you for a baby but I was wrong."

Snell looked him straight in the eye. Before Tom could say anything in reply, the Corporal stood up and walked back to his place in the ranks. He stared after his . . . friend? No, never a friend like Paddy. But he felt strangely proud that Snell and his tough cronies finally accepted him. Somehow, the thought of the upcoming attack wasn't quite as frightening now.

The Captain, looking very anxious, and Uncle Jim looking grim, returned to the company. Lashbrooke nervously reached for his water bottle – that was no longer there. He sighed and fingered the bit of broken cap that still dangled from the cord at his belt. He was not as intimidating now, standing in the rain, muddy, looking for his rum. Tom lifted his own arm up and sniffed the sleeve. The downpour had washed most of the rum out of his tunic.

Finally Lashbrooke straightened his shoulders, and pulled his sword out of his belt. The scabbard was useless – bent almost in half by the enemy bullet. He strode to the front of the Company.

"Here's the form, men, listen closely. The artillery will fire as fast as possible for the next ten minutes. The instant they stop, the infantry will rush the bottom of the ravine and drive the rebels out of the woods into the open where they will be captured or shot down."

He paused to twirl his moustache curls.

"G Company will be the centre of the attack. We must press home the assault with pluck and dash. I know that I can. . . ."

Tom checked his bugle and reseated the mouthpiece. Rain hammered on the brass rim.

" . . .a great day in the history of the 90th Battalion, Winnipeg Rifles. Carry on Sergeant Major."

Uncle Jim marched nearly to the lip of the ravine.

"Right Marker! G Company, fall in — two ranks."

The men hustled into position. Tom jogged to Captain Lashbrooke's side and stood at ease.

"G Company will fix bayonets!" Forty hands slapped bayonet handles, then slid the knives out of their holders in unison. The glittering blades were held poised beside forty rifles.

"Bayonets!" The bayonets snapped simul-taneously; Tom started at the sinister clicking noise. Uncle Jim walked both ranks. Each man's bayonet and cartridge pouch were checked.

They were ready. Two lines of dark green uniforms standing quietly in the rain, clutching their rifles, wait-ing for the command to advance. The artillerymen were hopping about their guns, feverishly loading and firing the last few shots before the attack. The sickening sulphur odour of gunpowder hung heavy in the air. Tom's stomach clenched in a painful spasm. Fear? Or Snell's beef?

The rain suddenly stopped, and a thin ray of sun burst through the clouds. The shaft of light caught the last bit of rain to make a rainbow arch right over the smouldering farmhouse. The cannons stopped firing. The wind calmed, and as if giving thanks for the beauty of the moment, a meadowlark trilled its song. Was it the same bird from the morning? The bird that started the battle? That lark seemed to signal the start of each round of fighting, just like his trumpet.

It was quiet now. Captain Lashbrooke fidgeted with his sword and watched intently for Major Boswell's signal. The ground in front of them sloped gently downward to the tangled bush and trees that lined the creek bed. Stretches of water showed here and there through the poplars where the creek meandered. To the right, all the artillerymen who didn't actually work on the guns were waiting with rifles and bayonets to join the attack as infantrymen. They stood on the edge of a sheer drop, twenty feet to the creek below.

Their line rippled and moved. Then the sound of the artillery bugler reached Tom. The music drew the gunners forward. The officer in front was waving his sword and shouting to the men. Amazingly, the officer then turned and ran full tilt over the edge of the hill. The men, like a herd, followed him and pitched over the brink in a floundering tangle of arms, legs, and rifles.

"Hurrah! The artillery!" Lashbrooke bellowed. "What gallant chaps, stout fellows all!"

Lashbrooke raised his sword expectantly and looked toward Major Boswell. The Major made no move but stood calmly, gazing at his watch. G Company began to jostle about.

"Steady! Hold still blast you!" Jim's command checked them. They were staring intently at their Captain's sword, waiting for it to drop. Tom remembered a hunting trip with his father and some rich Hudson Bay Company men. There had been a pack of hounds baying and howling, straining at the ends of their leash, waiting to be set loose on the trail of a coyote.

Uncle Jim's voice barked out again, steadying the men. Major Boswell glanced up from his watch. "Captain Lashbrooke! I'd be obliged if you would hold your men in check. We will attack only at the appointed time, not before, Sir!"

The Captain's face flushed red. He whirled around to face the men.

"I'm damned if the artillery will get all the glory. G Company doesn't wait for anybody. Bugler, sound the advance!"

Tom hesitated, surely he wasn't serious? They couldn't just disobey an order.

"SOUND the advance," Lashbrooke thundered.

Tom put the horn to his lips. The first notes were greeted by a cheer from the men as they surged forward like a green wave washing down the broad slope. Lashbrooke was waving his sword so wildly that twice Tom had to duck out of the path of the swinging blade. The men were shouting and yelling, but their ranks were steady. The Sergeant Major was like a sheep dog running to and fro, nipping at the slower men and curbing the fast ones to keep the herd in control. Off to the right a series of shots cracked, followed closely by the sound of men shouting commands, then more shots.

G Company was nearly to the bottom of the hill and so far had drawn no fire. That was good, at least they wouldn't be sitting ducks this time. Tom looked back; the other two companies with Major Boswell were now coming on behind them. Surely the enemy would retreat when they saw such a large force charging into their midst?

They reached some dense willow bushes and Captain Lashbrooke hacked a path through them with his sword. Tom followed. They broke free and found themselves perched atop the bank of the creek. It was only a few feet wide and without hesitation Lashbrooke waded into it. Tom lifted his bugle over his head and jumped, landing with a splash. The cold water surged up to his waist, and the shock took his breath away. He hurried forward and found the creek was deeper than he had thought, almost up to his armpits. The opposite bank was so steep that he had to go on his hands and knees slipping in the greasy mud until he caught hold of a bush on the top and pulled himself out.

He faced another solid tangle of willow and choke cherry bushes. Tom held his hands in front of his face and pushed into the snarled mass of branches. The twigs snagged his trumpet, tugged at his buttons, and hooked on his trousers. Only by physically throwing himself forward could he make any headway.

Suddenly, he burst out into a tiny patch of open ground surrounded by a thick stand of poplars. The Captain, muddy, streaming water, stood waiting for him. The rifle fire, now loud and threatening, seemed to be coming from their front. The shouts and screams of the artillerymen echoed through the dense trees. It was impossible to tell exactly where they were fighting.

The quiet glade was eerie, the sounds of the nearby battle were almost ghostly. The small hairs on the back of Tom's neck stood straight up. The rest of the Company was splashing in the creek behind them and presently some of the men came crashing through the bush.

"Right lads! This way! Follow me!" The Captain struck off along a narrow trail that offered entry into the poplars. The path wound first right, then to the left, then it disappeared altogether. Undaunted, Lashbrooke pushed on, veering right toward the sound of the shooting. They blundered on through the bush; the Captain let every branch whip back to catch Tom in the face. How could they be lost in such a small place? The whole coulee couldn't be more than one hundred and fifty yards wide.

Soon the trees thinned out and they found themselves on an open piece of grass alongside the creek again. The Captain stopped and glared around trying to get his bearings. Were they going around in circles? A huge smear of mud stretched from one cheek, across his nose to the other cheek. His face was scratched and one of his moustache curls dangled limp and wet on his chin while the other stood straight up. It would have been funny, any other time.

It sounded as though the fighting was all around them but exactly how to find the firing line was a mystery. G Company caught up to them and milled around on the small bank waiting for orders.

"*Wham, Wham, Wham!*"

Three shots split the air directly in front of them, the gun smoke burst through the dense bush on the other side of the creek.

A man beside Tom dropped with a grunt. Captain Lashbrooke yelped and leapt for the trees. Tom was right on his heels. The other men flung themselves to the ground and scrambled for cover, two of them quickly returning fire across the creek.

"Stop firing you idiots! They're 90th! They're Winnipeg boys," bellowed Uncle Jim from farther back in the trees. His Uncle's long legs came crashing through the undergrowth. He ran to the stream and yelled again for the men on the other side to stop firing. Three men in dark green uniforms stepped out of the bush on the opposite bank.

"Fools! I'll have you on charges for this!" Lashbrooke dashed to the edge of the creek, shaking his fist. The whole scene dissolved into a confusion of shouting, pushing men. The injured soldier had been lucky.

The bullet had hit him a glancing blow, just grazing his head. He had a nasty cut and a lump, but that was all.

Eventually they got themselves sorted out and with the Sergeant Major guiding, they moved off once more in the direction of the shooting. They broke clear of the poplar trees and found themselves pushing through tall grass and reeds that were nearly over Tom's head. The sound of the shooting was much closer and they could clearly hear the artillery officers giving orders off to their right. The invisible enemy might be anywhere. A lump of fear rose in Tom's throat as he walked slowly forward.

* * *

Luc heard the English voice; it couldn't be more than thirty yards away.

"Slow down, Men. Watch your front. They'll be close now."

There was no need to translate into French for Pierre, they both crouched lower in their trench and gripped their rifles. They'd been expecting the Englishmen to attack over the top of the ravine. It had come as a shock to hear the enemy moving up behind them on the other side of the creek. The firing was heavy off to their left but no enemy had appeared in their area yet.

They concentrated on the tall reeds. There was nothing to see but there was lots of noise; English voices, and the clatter of men tramping through the undergrowth. It sounded as though there were thousands of them. The temptation to shoot was great, but Pierre said they must hold their fire and make the first shot count.

"Are you certain this isn't some wild goose chase, Sergeant Major? Where are these rebels anyway? I think we should move farther to the right." The voice was loud, close. Luc squashed himself lower.

"If they're here we'll find 'em soon enough, Sir," a deep voice answered. "We have to make sure the artillery flank is clear. It sounds as though they're having a tough time of it."

Pierre smiled grimly. "Like buffalo Luc," he whispered. "We will catch them by surprise."

Luc could not feel so confident. In addition to themselves, there were only the two men hiding in the creek in front of them and three others off to their left hidden in another cattle rut. How could such a few hope to defeat so many? There was no place for them to escape. If they tried to move up the side of the ravine now they would be spotted and shot down or blown to pieces by the cannons. They had no choice but to fight it out here.

The memory of the dark woods at the Crossing flooded his imagination. He felt like a hunted animal, trapped. The sound of the trampling feet approached closer. He gripped his rifle until his knuckles turned white and clenched his teeth to keep them from chattering. He touched his sash, feeling the outline of the embroidered horse.

Suddenly a flash of sunlight reflecting from steel sparkled through the tall reeds. Then another and another until a whole line of long curved blades protruded up above the cattails. They were attached to the ends of rifles held up high. They seemed to be suspended, floating forward like a bizarre parade. Then the soldiers, dozens of them, were everywhere, only twenty yards away. Luc had a quick impression of faces, mostly young men, many with side whiskers, some smiling and talking, some muddy and tired.

"Kill the black devils!" bellowed Pierre. His rifle exploded - Luc flinched. One of the soldiers, a tall thin man, crumpled and fell in a heap. The other Métis nearby fired, almost as one. Soldiers were dropping everywhere, Luc couldn't tell which had been hit and which were simply taking cover.

He squinted down his own gun. There were dark uniforms leaping and running in and out of his sights — just like a swarm of black devils. He pulled the trigger and one of them disappeared in the cloud of smoke. He dropped down, fumbling for his powder flask, desperate to reload before they could get to him with those long wicked knives.

The rifle was awkward to handle in their shallow hole. If only they'd built the barricade on *this* side of the path! He spilled powder, fumbled with the ball, and finally got it rammed down the barrel. Rifles were banging and crashing constantly. Pierre had reloaded and fired twice more. The soldiers' bullets were buzzing

overhead, slapping into the trees, and one hit the log wall
behind them.

Luc waited until the shooting slowed down a bit,
then cautiously slid his rifle barrel up over the edge of
the rut and peeked out. All he could see on the far side
of the creek was the tall brown grass, trampled down in
spots, and Pierre's victim. He lay motionless like a bundle
of old rags, but no other soldier was visible.

An enemy rifle fired off to Luc's right. He could see
the wisps of smoke, and gingerly shifted his own sights
to cover the spot. He waited, trying to control the
trembling in his hands. A moment later there was some
movement, a flash of black uniform showed through the
grass then disappeared. Luc corrected his aim a fraction.
He only had to wait a second before the rifle fired again.
He saw the smoke, his sight post rested exactly on target.
He pulled the trigger.

Bang! Bang! two shots rang out opposite and both
bullets smashed into the logs behind Luc, only inches
from his head. He dropped to the bottom of his trench,
gasping with fright. Somebody on the other side was
playing the same game, shooting at *his* smoke.

Luc reloaded and carefully peeped up over the
trench. "Let your prey do the moving. Let him make the
mistakes." Father's advice.

He took aim on the same spot as before and watched.
Pierre was firing much more slowly, as were the other
Métis and the soldiers. Each side waited for a glimpse of
the other like a deadly game of tag. The sun was stronger

now but it scarcely reached Luc's hiding place. He shivered in his wet, muddy clothes and concentrated on his aim.

The uniform flashed in the tall grass again. Luc swivelled his gun barrel to follow the movement. The uniform appeared again; this time he could see it clearly. An arm or leg moving rapidly. Then he saw the whole soldier, on his stomach, crawling on his elbows and knees. He had almost disappeared again when Luc fired. This time he didn't wait to see what happened but ducked down under cover just as the two English bullets snapped overhead. Someone from the other side of the creek bellowed in pain.

* * *

"I have a vision of battle in which the men of Winnipeg will earn everlasting glory." The words echoed in Tom's mind. He remembered how grand they had sounded only two months ago when Captain Lashbrooke had spoken them. He looked around and realized that the glory he had envisioned, dashing charges on a heroic battlefield, was a far cry from the real thing.

There lay Harry Flett, the clerk at the Portage Loan and Savings Company where his father banked back home. Flett, who had always been so fussy and neat in the bank, now lay crumpled like a deflated accordion. His clothes, soaking wet and streaked with mud, covered his body like a tattered old tent that had collapsed in a storm.

They had been totally surprised by the rebel ambush. The first shot had caught Harry with a horrible thump in the chest and killed him outright. Tom, only a few feet away, lay flat in the dense reeds and cursed the enemy who always fired from hidden ambushes.

It was frustrating, shooting at a movement or a noise. Near the creek, Snell crawled out of the reeds into the grass on his elbows and knees trying to get a better view of the concealed enemy. He was desperate to shoot back.

"WHACK."

Snell's head snapped back. He rolled over, clutching his jaw, bellowing in rage and pain. The Corporal retreated quickly to Tom's position.

"They hit me! On the chin!"

"Is it bad?"

"Hurts like the devil, but I can still move my jaw. Here, have a look and bandage it for me." Snell pulled a handkerchief from his pocket and gave it to Tom. He thrust his face forward.

Tom recoiled in disgust. The bullet had torn a deep gouge through the flesh exactly on the tip of Snell's chin. The blood welled up red and horrible in the gash. He folded the cloth into a narrow bandage, placed the thickest part against the wound, and wrapped the two ends around the top of Snell's head where he tied them tightly. The Corporal winced with pain and clenched his teeth but his eyes shone, bright as fire. Tom knew the fire was pure hatred.

"Kill 'em!" Snell muttered through his bloodied lips. "I swear I'll kill one with my own hand before this day is out."

He was a fearsome sight, more animal than human. He flicked the Snider's breech cover open, fed in a new cartridge and slapped the cover shut in one smooth motion. Then he crawled back through the tall grass toward the creek.

There was one other wounded man; Tom didn't know him very well. Including Smitty and Flaherty, G Company now had four casualties — five if you counted Snell — and they still had yet to see a single enemy, much less hit one. Some of the men lay flat and hardly lifted up to fire a shot or look for the enemy. Others, like Snell, were boiling mad and shot at anything that moved. Lashbrooke was resting on one elbow gazing around as though in a stupor; all the energy seemed to have gone out of him.

Uncle Jim was helping bandage up the other wounded man. At least they still had his uncle; he would get them out of this. The old Jim, always full of jokes and stories was gone now, replaced by the tough, efficient Sergeant Major who seemed to know just what to do no matter how bad things got.

Tom felt better, looking at him. He knew the old Uncle Jim was still in there, but right now they needed a good soldier, not jokes. When the wounded man had been taken care of, Jim crawled over to the Captain.

"Judging by their fire, I don't reckon there's more than a half dozen or so," his uncle spoke slowly and quietly. "If we could get a few men upstream around that bend; they could cross over and come up behind the rebel pits."

The Captain roused himself with an obvious effort. "Who do you propose for this expedition, Sergeant Major?" he asked with little enthusiasm.

"Myself, Corporal Snell, Tom here, and three others should do it."

Tom's ears perked up at the mention of his name. "What on earth do you plan to do man? Snell is wounded, and the boy can't shoot anyone with a bugle. Don't be ridiculous." The Captain shut his eyes and lay back against the reeds.

"We'll just scare 'em out into the open where the rest of the company can get a good shot in, Sir," Jim explained patiently. "We'll work around them, like I said. Then when we're in position I'll get Tom here to sound the advance and the rest of us will start shooting like the blazes. . . ."

"Yeeees, quite," the Captain interrupted, sitting up suddenly bright-eyed. "I see your idea. The rebels will think they're being attacked from behind. When they try to run for it we'll have them right in our sights."

"That's about it, Sir," Jim nodded.

"What if they don't move? You could be caught in a sticky situation yourself?"

"We'll just back out. They won't follow us, but if they try to you should be able to get a clear shot at them and pin them down until we get clear. Anyway, I figure it's our only chance to get a good lick in at these rebels. If we can get 'em moving we might roll up their whole line and clear the ravine."

The idea that G Company could win the day appealed to Lashbrooke because he immediately passed orders for the company to hold its fire until they heard the bugle call. Tom crawled off through the grass with his uncle, relieved that at last they had a plan to fight back.

Snell positively giggled with delight when he heard the plan and Jim had no problem finding three more volunteers. They gathered on either side of the Sergeant Major. He used a stick to scratch a picture of the creek and ravine in the earth. He marked exactly where they would go and whispered each man's instructions. He made them repeat the plan back to him.

They crawled out to the poplar trees then got up and ran, crouched over through the bush. The Sergeant Major led and the others followed in single file. They went about one hundred yards down the ravine, then stopped. On Jim's signal, all took cover while he crept off in the direction of the creek. He was soon back and looked satisfied.

"Now pay close attention," he hissed at them. "We're well beyond the bend in the creek and it looks clear but there may be more rebels hiding on the other bank. If we make so much as one bit of noise, they'll be on to us. Follow me, move only when I do, and for God's sake be quiet." He pressed his forefinger to his lips. "If we're ambushed it's every man for himself; get back as best you can."

Tom searched his Uncle's face for some recognition of the old Jim but found only the hard, fierce Sergeant Major. He would be expected to do his part like the other men; there would be no special treatment. The thought was chilling. But he resolved that whatever happened, Thomas Kerslake would not fail. They went on elbows and knees, rifles cradled in their arms, like a column of armed caterpillars.

Belly-crawling to the edge of the creek left Tom panting for breath. They paused briefly while Jim observed the other side of the creek for activity, then slid into the water. They crossed quickly, crouched so that only their heads and rifles were above the surface of the water. The icy cold hit Tom's heated body like a shock. First the rain, then two dunkings in the creek. It seemed ages since he had been dry and warm.

Tom felt horribly exposed here; anyone watching could shoot them down easily, but all remained quiet. They slithered up the opposite bank and crawled through the underbrush. When they were safely into the trees away from the creek, they halted.

"We'll have to hurry it up," his uncle whispered. "The longer we spend here, the more chance of being discovered."

He led them on in short spurts of running, from one piece of cover to another, bent over, always watching. They approached the bend in the creek and carefully followed it around until they could see the opposite bank where G Company waited. Flett's body lay in the trampled patch of grass and reeds. The rest of G Company was hidden from view. They dropped to their bellies and snaked forward inch by inch.

"Blam!" It was a rebel rifle, and just in front of them. An excited voice chattered in French. They froze and stared at the bushes where the shot had come from. The enemy was still invisible but now it was their turn to spring a surprise. Jim motioned for Tom to stay where he was, then led Snell and the other three men to positions in line with Tom so that all five of them could fire directly into the enemy position. He crawled back to Tom and whispered:

"All right, Tom! I don't want you to show yourself, stay down. Start playing and keep playing until I tell you to stop."

Suddenly Tom was nervous. With trembling hands he fitted the mouthpiece into the bugle and raised himself up on his elbows. He took a huge breath and blew. The trumpet notes blared out violently, calling on the imaginary army to advance.

"Open Fire!" Five rifles banged like a string of fire crackers.

"G Company, by platoon — Fire!"

Snell and the other men started shouting, reloading and shooting as fast as they could. Rifles from the company on the other side of the creek were going off, filling the air with noise. Over it all the high bugle notes rang out crisp and clear. Bits of bark flew from a couple of old logs down near the water where the soldiers' fire was concentrated.

Then, for the first time, Tom saw the enemy. They had been like ghosts but now, at last, he could see and believe that they were real flesh and blood. A lean figure leapt over the two old logs and rolled once on the ground. He came up like a cat weaving through the trees only scant yards away. Jim's rifle boomed; the enemy's right leg buckled backward at a grotesque angle throwing him to the ground. Tom caught a glimpse of a dark, hand- some face, screwed up in pain, coal black eyes and long, braided hair. Then he was gone, rolling behind a patch of willow.

"NOW! NOW, BOYS!" Snell's voice bellowed like a bull moose smothering even the sound of the bugle. Snell was on his feet, rifle and bayonet extended, racing toward the wounded rebel. Tom stopped blowing abrupt- ly, startled by the vision of the corporal, wet and tattered, handkerchief tied around his head like an old washer- woman, galloping through the trees screaming for blood.

"Snell, get down. DOWN, you fool!" The Sergeant Major's command checked him, but he didn't take cover. Snell's rifle flew up and he aimed directly into the willow.

Then Tom saw the second rebel. A small man appeared over the top of the two logs, his rifle pointed at Corporal Snell at nearly point blank range. There was no time to warn anyone, no time to think about it - he either acted, or Snell died. Tom was on his feet and running, a bullet from the other side of the river snapped past his ear. He put the trumpet to his lips and blew a screeching, piercing blast as loud as he could.

It wasn't a note, just a bugle howl but it worked; the little rebel swung away from Snell. The deadly rifle was now aimed at Tom. The small black hole in the muzzle stared him in the face. He braced for the shot that was certain to come as his last breath wheezed through the bugle.

* * *

Luc was in a frenzy; they were trapped! The bugle call had come as a complete surprise from behind them. Pierre reacted instantly. "Surrounded! We go now Luc!"

A hail of enemy bullets from all directions pounded their position; Luc had no time to argue or think.

"I'll draw their fire. When you hear me shoot, you get out. Go downstream to Delorme," Pierre shouted and then he was gone like a deer over the logs and up the hillside.

Luc had just poured a load of powder down his rifle. He jammed a ball in the muzzle and rammed it home. Then Pierre screamed. Luc stood and looked over the log wall. There was his friend, blood pumping from his smashed knee, white teeth gritted and bared, showing bright in his dark face – helpless. He heard the bull roar of the Englishman and saw the black-clad soldier with a white rag on his head charging down on Pierre. The long curved blade at the end of his rifle homed in relentlessly. Luc threw his rifle up onto the logs just as the soldier stopped. He couldn't miss, the front sight rested dead centre on his enemy's head.

A howling banshee, screaming like the devil, made Luc jump. He swerved to his left and saw a boy soldier running directly at him blowing a brass horn. The bugle! Here was that blasted horn that signalled the start of all the attacks! He would silence it right now.

He aimed, bullets cracked through the air around him and smacked into the logs. The horn shrieked and Pierre called out for him to run. He didn't care. He felt no fear, only cold hate. He would get the trumpet. Even as he pulled the trigger, a thought flashed through his mind: "The horn blowers are boys, like me!"

CLICK, the hammer fell but the rifle didn't fire. He yanked the hammer back and jerked the trigger again, still no shot. There was no percussion cap. He had loaded the gun but Pierre's scream had distracted him and he had forgotten the cap. Now it was hopeless. His caps were lying at the bottom of the trench, no time to retrieve one and fire.

The soldier boy had stopped blowing his horn and stood facing Luc only a foot from the end of the rifle. He looked stunned; he should have been dead. Luc suddenly felt tired. The hate drained from him and left him hollow.

"YAAAAAAHH!" Luc whirled around to see the strange soldier with the rag tied to his head leaping over the logs, the deadly bayonet thrusting for his chest. It was pure reflex that saved Luc's life.

He brought his rifle up, and at the last second, deflected the knife up over his head. The soldier whipped the butt end of his own rifle and drove it into Luc's stomach. Luc dropped like a stone; the wind driven completely out of him. He lay squirming on the ground doubled up in pain, desperately gulping for air. The big soldier stood over him, the bayonet poised to plunge into his throat.

Luc closed his eyes, and gasped, "Hail Mary, full of grace, the Lord is with thee." He could see his mother and Marie clearly. Then they faded and he was alone in the dark.

The blow never came. Slowly his gut relaxed and he drew a ragged breath of air. He opened his eyes. The boy was struggling with the big soldier, holding onto the barrel of the rifle while the soldier tried to shake him loose.

"No!" the boy yelled. "His rifle was empty; he's unarmed. You can't kill him. He's a prisoner."

The big soldier replied with a grunt and flung the boy away; then raised the bayonet to strike. The boy bounced up and threw a wild punch that clipped the soldier on his cheek, staggering him. Then it was over, an older soldier arrived.

"Corporal Snell!" the old soldier barked. "Put that away."

The rifle lowered reluctantly.

"Get the prisoner, and let's go! The 90th are pulling back; the attack is over. We have to get out now or we'll be left behind."

Luc was wrenched roughly to his feet. All the firing had stopped; he looked over to where Pierre lay, expecting the worst but Pierre was gone! A puddle of blood stained the dun-coloured grass. A trail of bright scarlet drips led downstream to the Métis positions. Pierre had escaped! He had saved Pierre! He rubbed his aching stomach and nodded at the boy soldier. "Merci, pour ma vie."

The boy looked puzzled, Luc smiled and said, "Thank you, for saving my life." The boy turned away.

8.   Capture

Tom, standing above the rebel trench, could see the other side of the creek easily. G Company was pulling back. The dark green uniforms were clearly visible, moving back through the deep grass toward the trees. Why weren't they waiting? It might still be dangerous to re-cross the creek here. Uncle Jim wanted to go back around the bend, the way they had come. He shouted across the creek:

"Captain Lashbrooke!"

From far away in the trees the answer came, "We're pulling back, Kerslake, the whole line! Get out of it or you'll be cut off."

"Wait! We need your covering fire," his uncle shouted. Tom, for the first time ever, detected a note of fear, even desperation, in his Uncle's voice.

Lashbrooke was even farther away now. "We can't wait, Kerslake. You're on your own!"

The Sergeant Major swore bitterly. It was quiet and forbidding in the dense undergrowth of the ravine. Were there Indian warriors already slinking back through the trees after them? Tom looked at their prisoner. He wasn't a small man, only a boy. His clothes were filthy and tattered and his eyes were red from exhaustion. Even so, he showed no emotion. In fact he looked proud and stubborn, not defeated or depressed at all.

There was something about the way he stood, stiff backed and chin up. Something familiar. The spy! Could it be the same young boy from Clark's Crossing? Tom studied the prisoner's face but that was no good — he hadn't seen the face at the Crossing. This boy was definitely bigger too — a small man he'd thought a minute ago. Paddy would know, but Paddy was lying unconscious, maybe dead. He'd have to ask Captain Lashbrooke.

"I don't like it but we'll have to cross here and catch up with the company as fast as we can," Jim announced. He fed a fresh cartridge into his rifle and snapped the breech shut.

"There may still be more rebels downstream. If so, they'll have a clear shot at us when we're in the water, so we have to move quick. Don't worry about noise or cover; don't stop for anything. When I give the word, it's everybody into the water and run like hell. Corporal Snell, if the prisoner gives any trouble, finish him."

Snell grinned like an animal; the point of his bayonet pricked the back of the rebel's neck. There was no doubt the mixed-blood boy understood English, but he showed no sign of fear at the threat. Tom caught his Uncle's eye. The grim Sergeant Major's face cracked, and for an instant his old uncle smiled at him.

"What if Violet could see you in her kitchen now eh, Tommy?"

Tom laughed. Covered in mud and streaming water, he could easily picture Violet's reaction if he appeared in her spotless kitchen. What were Vi and Father doing right now? Winnipeg seemed like a different world. If only he could see them — be there, just for a moment. He swallowed hard.

They moved to the edge of the creek and tensed themselves.

"Go!"

Tom took two running steps and jumped, landing in the middle of the stream; the other men hit the water beside him in a great splash. Tom lost his footing and went down, the water closed over his head. He floundered and came up spluttering and coughing. A rifle shot cracked and a spout of water erupted in front of him. The invisible enemy was still there; and he was a prize target.

He tried to run through the chest-deep water but it was like a nightmare. The harder he tried, the slower he went. The others were already at the bank, scrambling out of the water.

The prisoner slipped, or pretended to slip, off the bank back into the water. Snell's hand shot out and clamped onto the rebel's neck. The Corporal's powerful arm lifted him, wriggling like a jackfish, and threw him down on the shore.

"Move!" His bayonet jabbed, pricking the boy's leg. The prisoner bounded to his feet and ran, Snell's rifle inches behind him.

Another rifle shot banged and the slug thudded into the muddy shore of the creek, followed immediately by another that sprayed water into Tom's face. The familiar bark of the Snider Enfield sounded behind him. He glanced over his shoulder and saw his uncle standing in the middle of the creek, returning the enemy fire.

Then he was at the bank. He grabbed some reeds and flung himself up out of the water, stumbled, fell, regained his feet and was sprinting for the trees. Flett's body lay crumpled in front of him. He leaped, clearing it in a single bound, and kept running, not daring to look back. The slow-motion nightmare was gone, he flew over the uneven ground and into the trees. Snell, the prisoner, and the other soldiers were already there and moments later Jim came crashing through the brush.

"We made it!" Snell whooped at the top of his voice. He aimed his rifle back across the creek. "Take this, you red buggers!" And fired a shot.

The other men laughed with relief. Jim slapped Tom on the back, "Thank God you're alright Tom! I figured you for a goner when you went under. You picked a rotten time to go for a swim, boy!" Even the prisoner smiled.

They made good time back through the bush and recrossed the creek; this time at a place where it was only ankle deep. All the other Winnipeg Companies were back in their original positions at the top of the hill.

Most of G Company were sitting in small groups talking and smoking. Very few were in a proper firing line or even alert. Jim increased his pace coming up the hill. His face was set with the hard look of the Sergeant Major again. He strode up to the nearest group of men.

"Who told you the battle was over?" he barked. "Get off your lazy backsides and get into the firing line." The men scattered like rabbits to their positions.

Tom stayed with Snell and the prisoner, who had caused quite a stir. The men kept pointing and staring as though the rebel was a ghost suddenly appeared among them. Captain Lashbrooke, who had been talking to the artillery officers, soon came jogging up to them, a wide grin on his face.

"Welcome back, Sergeant Major! No trouble getting out, eh?," his voice positively oozed sweetness. Tom thought he would be sick. Lashbrooke runs out on them, and now when they show up safe, he thinks he can smooth it all over as though nothing had happened.

Uncle Jim saluted the Captain formally. "Actually we had a great deal of difficulty getting out, Sir." His voice would have cracked ice. Lashbrooke pretended not to notice.

"I see, but no point in worrying about it now. All's well that ends well! No harm done, eh, Sergeant Major?" he beamed and put his hand on Jim's shoulder. Jim looked at the hand as though his eyes would burn holes in it. Tiny jaw muscles twitched as he gritted his teeth. The hand dropped quickly.

"No harm done, Sir," Jim replied, his tone was menacing. "But if you had stayed just a few minutes to give us covering fire we could have crossed the creek farther down in safety."

Lashbrooke's face turned crimson; he shrank back a step. "We had orders from the artillery, they were pulling back so we had to. There was no time to wait, don't you see?"

"NO TIME!" Jim exploded. "Good God, Man! That whole attack only lasted twenty minutes! What difference would a few more minutes have made! We had them moving! If you had kept the pressure up we could've pushed 'em right out of the ravine."

"But the artillery were leaving. . . ." the Captain tried lamely, but Jim cut him off.

"You should have told them to stay put. If the bloody artillery had stuck their ground, this battle would be finished. Now we'll have to go down and start all over." Jim's tone had changed to one of a school teacher scolding a student. Lashbrooke for once had nothing to say; he simply stood tugging nervously at his moustache curls.

In spite of the disgust he felt for Lashbrooke, Tom was sorry for him. He knew what it felt like to get chewed out. It must have been doubly humiliating for a grown man. A long silence ensued in which the Captain was unable to look any of them in the eye. Eventually, Jim softened his voice.

"Anyway, we wounded one and took this prisoner. The wounded rebel crawled off into the bush; we couldn't find him. We should let the General see this boy. He speaks English and may give us some information."

Lashbrooke looked tremendously relieved. "Yes, yes, yes! Excellent work, Sergeant Major!" he babbled. "I'm sure the General will be very pleased to see a prisoner, pleased indeed."

Tom slipped in beside the Captain. "Sir," he whispered. "Do you recognize the prisoner?"

Lashbrooke looked at Tom as though he'd gone crazy.

"Recognize him? What in God's name are you talking about?"

The prisoner glanced at them.

"I think he might be the same boy as at the Crossing."

The Captain waved Tom away. "You're imagining things. That was a child at the Crossing. This is an enemy warrior — G Company doesn't capture children."

"But Sir. . . ."

"Be quiet!" He brushed past Tom. "Here comes the General now. I have to report."

They all snapped to attention; Lashbrooke saluted. General Middleton and one of his aides reined in beside the Captain.

"Hot work, Lashbrooke," the General greeted them. He gazed down from atop his horse. "How did you fare?"

The Captain had recovered his composure and answered brightly. "Pretty well, sir. We lost one killed and another wounded but we gave 'em a good dose of lead and had them on the run, in fact. Pity the artillery boys decided to pull out. I think we could have cleared the ravine with a bit more determination on their part."

Tom almost burst. The nerve of the man! He looked to Jim, but his uncle just stood like a stone at attention. The little jaw muscles were twitching again.

"We did manage to capture one of the rascals, Sir," Lashbrooke continued in his best lawyer's voice. "Put up the devil of a struggle he did, but we prevailed."

The General nudged his horse over a few feet to where the prisoner and Snell were standing. "Well done, Captain. Very well done!"

"Yes sir, he even speaks English. I thought he might give us some useful information. That's why I was so keen to get him back alive."

The bald-faced liar! Tom felt he had to speak even if his Uncle didn't. Jim remained silent. How could he let Lashbrooke take all the credit? The General leaned down over the neck of his horse for a closer look at the rebel. Corporal Snell, still wearing his head bandage, stepped quickly between the general and the prisoner.

"Beg your pardon, General," he said. "But the Captain was right. This little 'un is dangerous. He never run like the others; fought us right to the end. Had to knock him down myself. But it wasn't the Captain that took him, it was me and the Sergeant Major and the bugler here. The Captain made it sound like he did all the work, but that's just a pile of horse apples. He couldn't wait to get outta there! Left us for dead if you want the truth General."

"You impertinent fool!" Lashbrooke screeched. "How dare you speak like that to the General! You'll lose your stripes by God!"

"Don't care. What I said is the truth. Anything else is a plain lie," Snell replied evenly.

"That's done it! That's insubordination by heaven! I'll have you court-martialled and broken, Snell." Lashbrooke's face was crimson; little bits of spittle flew from his lips. He turned to Jim, "Sergeant Major, arrest that man and take him away."

Tom could take no more. "NO! Corporal Snell's telling the truth, General. You can't arrest him!" his voice trembled.

"Nobody shall be arrested," the General said firmly. "This is a most unseemly squabble and it will cease immediately."

"But Sir!" Lashbrooke rushed to the General and seized the horse's bridle. "I can't be expected to listen to this, I'm. . . ."

"If you please, Captain Lashbrooke!" The General jerked on the reins, his horse pranced backward. "I am still trying to fight a battle. We'll not be stopping to convene any court-martial for something said in the heat of the moment."

"But — but — the blackguard's insulted me!" Lashbrooke spluttered.

"He's also brought you a prisoner, so we'll call it square, eh, Captain," the General replied with a smile.

"All right by me, General," Snell piped up. The Captain threw him a dirty look. The General laughed loudly.

"Deliver the prisoner to the *zareba*. Captain Whitla will hold him there for me to interrogate later. Carry on Lashbrooke! Back to the fray!"

The General and his aide, wearing a big smirk, rode off toward the artillery who had just opened fire again. As they left Tom overheard the General. "Militia! Keen to fight I dare say, but deuced difficult to control."

The Captain glared at Tom first, then Snell. The General's word was law. "What an infernal humbug this is," he finally grumbled. "Alright Sergeant Major, you heard the General. Get rid of the prisoner." He stomped off, ruthlessly tugging on his moustache curls.

The Sergeant Major detailed five men to go with Corporal Snell and the prisoner back to the *zareba*. They would pick up more ammunition from the wagons after they had dropped off the prisoner.

"Tom, I want you to go with them. Wait at the *zareba* with the prisoner and Captain Whitla. Tell him I told you to stay there. He's a good man; he'll take care of you."

"But I'm needed here!" Tom protested. "I'm the company bugler. What's the matter?"

"Nothing's wrong, Tom. You're one of my best men, but I'm sorry I let you get involved in any of this." His Uncle Jim, not the Sergeant Major, smiled at him.

"These rebels are going to make a fight of it; things could get a lot worse. I won't have you near the Captain. Not now, not in his mood. I've seen men like him do crazy things, Tom, and I don't want him to take you along. If he makes any trouble I'll handle it. Now get going!"

There was no point in arguing. Snell and the others had already moved off; he ran after them. As it turned out, G Company did no more fighting that day, and somehow Captain Lashbrooke found a fresh bottle of rum, so he consoled himself with it and caused no trouble.

* * *

The *zareba* the English soldiers kept talking about
turned out to be nothing more than a rough circle of
wagons with the horses and mules corralled inside.
Exactly the same as a Métis hunting camp. There was
only one tent and it was being used as a hospital. There
were wounded men lying crowded around it. Luc's
guard, the man named Snell, marched them over to it,
then went inside. Luc waited outside with the trumpet
player, Tom, and the other men.

He was astonished at the number of wounded
soldiers. He started counting but quit with an uneasy
feeling when he reached twenty. Many of them lay
wrapped in blankets on small beds of willow branches
while others were bundled up in coats and parkas. Most
were quiet but several were groaning and crying. It was
hard to listen to. Three lay side by side sprawled on the
ground with no cover at all. He realized with a jolt that
they were dead. One corpse stared directly at him, the
vacant eyes almost accusing Luc of the young man's
death. Luc shuddered and looked the other way.

The sunlight had once again vanished behind a
shroud of heavy grey clouds. A violent gust of cold wind
started the tent flapping and Luc looked up to the sky
praying it would not rain again. It didn't, but seconds
later the hail came. It only lasted a couple of minutes but

it was furious and pounded them with stinging white stones. The wounded men muttered and swore at the added pain.

Luc wondered about Pierre with his smashed knee, still back there in the ravine hiding from the cannon fire. There was no doctor for him and no shelter from the hail either. Would he ever see his friend's smiling face again? The thought of escape crossed his mind for the first time. Not now, surrounded by soldiers in broad daylight, but later at night, perhaps.

Snell emerged from the tent with an officer.

"Thank you, carry on Corporal."

Snell and the officer saluted. Snell turned to leave and their eyes met; Luc was startled by the hatred in those eyes. This soldier would kill him without pity given half a chance.

The officer put Luc in the back of a covered wagon and assigned two of his own soldiers as guards.

The wagon was packed with crates wrapped in burlap and marked "BISCUIT". The thought of food made his mouth water. The soldiers had been careless, they had never properly searched him so he still had his pocket knife. Cutting the burlap cover he pried up one of the boards from the top of the crate and found it full of smaller tin boxes. The tins contained pieces of hard flat bread.

He bit ravenously on one and grunted with pain; the biscuit was like stone. He chipped a piece off with his knife and put the whole chunk in his mouth. In a few seconds it softened enough for him to chew. It wasn't very tasty but it felt good to have food in his stomach again. He ate two biscuits, then lay back on top of the crates. Outside, the gunfire was increasing to a full-pitched roar and moments later rain started to beat on the wagon cover. For the first time in two full days he was safe, fed, and out of the rain. He fell into a deep sleep.

"Get that half-breed rebel! He can do some work for us."

Luc sat up, rubbing his eyes. Where was he? Yes, a prisoner in the Englishmen's *zareba*. One of the guards came in and roughly shoved him outside into the rain. It was late afternoon; he must have been asleep for at least three hours.

The camp was in an uproar. Men were running everywhere. Teamsters were hitching up their wagons and it seemed that every soldier was shouting orders at every other soldier. The guard led Luc over to the hospital tent where he was put to work pulling the crates and stores out of some of the wagons. As soon as he had a wagon emptied, the soldiers lifted the wounded men in and laid them on the floor. One of the soldiers helping with the wounded was the bugler, Tom. Their eyes met and they nodded in recognition.

The wagons were eventually assembled into line and they started off toward the Saskatchewan River. Luc and his guards trudged along beside the hospital wagons. There was almost no shooting to be heard. He looked over to the ravine. It was thickly lined with soldiers but very few of them were firing. Most were lying well back from the edge.

In addition to the dark green riflemen there were now hundreds of soldiers in scarlet coats. They must have arrived after he had been taken prisoner. There were also two more cannons. They must be preparing for an attack and with that many men how could they fail to wipe out the few poorly armed Métis and Indians left in the coulee?

Tom was riding up with the driver on the wagon nearest Luc. "Will you attack now and kill all my friends?"

Tom looked away.

"Please, is the battle over? Are any Métis still alive?"

"Why should I tell you anything?" Tom snapped. "Your friends are the killers; they deserve what they get."

"If so, then why did you save my life?" Luc persisted.

Tom said nothing for a moment, then with a sigh, he answered. "No, we're not going to attack. It's over, we're pulling back to make a fortified camp. Your friends have escaped this time."

Luc's heart leaped. They did it! The tiny Métis army had fought off the soldiers! His friends were alive to fight another day. They might yet send this English army back in defeat. Luc grinned and picked up his step. He would surely be able to escape and rejoin his people. He touched his sash and felt the outline of the little horse, his lucky

talisman was still working. And just to be on the safe
side he said a short prayer of thanksgiving.

Over the next few days Luc never had time to think
of escaping, much less attempt it. The soldiers showed
no sign of moving on, and worked to improve their camp
by the river. Every day he was roused before dawn and
worked for the cooks chopping wood, hauling water, and
cleaning up. Then he was sent to help dig trenches, or
latrines, or shift stores for the rest of the day so that by
nightfall he was so tired he fell dead asleep. During the
day his guards never left him and at night a sentry was
stationed permanently by his side.

The soldiers spent a lot of time drilling. The
cannons were fascinating. He'd actually talked to
Lieutenant Rivers, one of the artillery officers, and
learned how the things worked. The artillerymen
manoeuvred their big guns as skillfully as he handled his
little rifle. One day they fired at targets a thousand yards
away, smashing them to pieces. How had he and Pierre
ever survived?

They were also very determined. The English army
had lost many men killed and over forty wounded yet
they were still full of spirit and talked confidently about
how they would fight the next battle. Were his comrades
preparing as well?

Each day Luc expected to be interrogated, and he
had rehearsed what he would say so as not to betray any
secrets. Yet only those soldiers curious to see an "enemy"
had come to see him. He saw the bugler, Tom, several

times and even talked to him once. Each day was the same, hard labour and close guard. But not today.

He had just finished cleaning up for the cooks when one of the General's aides came to get him. They went to a tent next door to the General's and chatted for a few minutes. The aide, Captain Freer, asked Luc about his family and home, but not about the Métis army.

The tent flap lifted. "Hello little rebel, how's number two been treating you?"

It was Lieutenant Rivers, looking very smart in his best uniform.

"Number two? What is that?"

Rivers sat down beside him. "Not what — who. Freer here, he's number two." Both men laughed. Luc smiled hesitantly. Were they making fun of him?

"Sorry, Reb." The artilleryman nodded at his friend. "Captain Freer and I joined the army together years ago. He was given number two — I was number ten."

"Like the little black devils? They are number ninety, right?"

Now the soldiers looked puzzled. "Little black devils? What are you talking about?"

"The soldiers from Winnipeg, the 90th — in the black uniforms. When they attacked us, if one went down, it didn't matter. They just kept coming, like little devils. My friend called them black devils."

The Englishmen burst out laughing. "Excellent! Perfect name for the Rifles. Little Black Devils! By God they'll love that. Maybe we won't tell 'em; they'll be so conceited."

Luc laughed with them. Then Rivers stood. "But enough of this. We're ready outside, just give me a second." He left the tent. Captain Freer pulled the tent flap back and motioned for Luc to look out.

"Tell me, do you recognize that man?" he asked.

Luc was baffled. Three men stood talking a short distance from the tent. One was Rivers. The second man was short, had a big belly, and long white moustaches. Luc remembered him easily from the day of the battle. "Yes, that's your general."

"Of course," the aide said, smiling. "But what about the other one?"

Luc looked again. What kind of trick were they trying to play on him? The third man was tall, heavy, and had long curly black hair sticking out from under an old slouch hat. His back was turned to Luc. He wore a deer hide jacket, patched trousers, and moccasins. Moccasins, not boots. That was strange. Maybe he was one of the scouts. The man suddenly turned away from the general, laughing loudly. Luc had a glimpse of the face; it was all he needed.

"Larouche!" he gasped.

"Is he one of your men?"

Luc was stunned, and answered without thinking. "Yes, yes, he was with us at the battle but deserted us, the coward, and now he talks to the General like an old friend!"

"Good, we didn't know if he could be trusted. He came here claiming he could spy for us. Says he deserted the rebel camp. Demanded a lot of money for his services. We thought he might have been sent by Riel to bring us false information. From what you've just said, it would appear he's telling the truth."

"He's a bully and a coward! He wouldn't know the truth to tell it," Luc said bitterly, his eyes glued to Larouche who was laughing again for the General's benefit. Like a dog licking boots.

"Do you know what?" Freer dropped the canvas flap. "I agree with you my little rebel. I think he's a scoundrel and a liar. I wouldn't trust a man who would sell out his own people either. Anyway, he's to stay with us now."

Luc shook his head. Didn't Larouche know that even the English soldiers despised traitors? And Marie! What would happen to her? Was she safe with the priests or would Riel punish her for her father's treachery?

"What about his family? Has he left them?" he asked the officer.

"Why no, now that you mention it, he brought his wife and daughter in with him today. They're in a tent at the west end of the camp. Do you know them?"

Luc's head reeled. Marie, here in the same camp only a hundred yards away! "Yes," he mumbled. "They're good people; they're my friends."

The aide smiled. "Come on then. Can't do any harm now; you're not going anywhere."

He led Luc out of the tent, past the General and Larouche who didn't even notice them. It was unbelievable. Here was Larouche speaking to the General in the middle of the enemy camp. He still couldn't believe it; not even a brute like Larouche could be so treacherous.

They crossed to the west side of the camp and arrived at a stained and patched old tent. Mme. Larouche was there, preparing some food in a kettle suspended above a small fire. Marie knelt beside her, stirring the pot. Her light brown hair, braided neatly in a single plait reflected the afternoon sun. Luc stood tongue-tied, staring at the strong, slim face. Marie looked up from her work and the colour drained from her cheeks. She crossed herself, "Maman!"

"What's wrong? It's me, Luc Goyette," he stammered.

"They said you were dead," Marie gaped, as if she still didn't believe her eyes. Then she was on her feet, running to him and in a second she was holding him tightly. Luc could feel her crying, sobs shaking her body, but he was ecstatic. He was floating on a cloud! She really did care for him! She was crying for him! He was happy and at peace and strangely, felt tears stinging his own eyes. The fear, hardship, fighting, capture — none of it mattered so much any more.

"Pierre said that you saved his life, that you stayed behind to fight the soldiers and that they killed you while he escaped," her voice quivered.

Luc was suddenly full of questions. "Is Pierre alright? Do my parents think I'm dead? How many survived the battle?"

Marie answered. Pierre's wound had given him a fever that lasted three days and almost killed him but he had survived it and the wound was now clean. She had helped nurse him at the priest's rectory. She hadn't seen his parents for days. There had been four Métis killed in the battle; Paranteau he already knew. In addition young Boyer, old Monsieur Vermette, and Michel Desjarlais had all died. Also, a Cree from One Arrow's reserve had been killed but she didn't know his name.

"But your father — he's betrayed us! What will happen to you?" Marie's mother covered her face with her hands and rushed into the tent. Marie bowed her head in shame.

"I don't know, Luc. We left Batoche yesterday but we didn't know he was taking us to the enemy camp. Maman won't leave him, but I will. I have to — I can't stay here."

Captain Freer called, "Time to go young rebel."

He whispered hastily, "Don't worry. We'll escape together; I'll think of something."

As he walked away, he pulled the embroidered horse from his waist band and held it up so Marie could see it. She smiled and his heart soared.

9.   Escape

Hail, the conquering hero comes!"

Tom blushed. Corporal Snell and his friends laughed at his embarrassment. But the laughter was good natured, and Tom shouted back at them.

"The bugle is mightier than the sword, Corporal!"

Tom hurried on, glad to be free of Snell. The Corporal no longer bullied him, in fact the opposite was true. Since Tom had risked his life for Snell, he had become too friendly. Snell had taken over as an unofficial protector for Tom, always doing him favours, and helping him with his work. The whole situation was unnatural and uncomfortable. Snell was still the rough, rude, violent man that Tom disliked. It was hard to accept his friendship.

He and Snell had become very popular in the camp. The story of Snell's bayonet charge — and Tom's bugle charge, was fast becoming a regimental legend. He'd told and retold the story many times but men still stopped him to ask about it. The capture of the rebel was one of the few success stories to come out of the battle.

Tom felt like a fraud whenever the story was told. Everyone thought he was extremely brave, but he remembered looking down the barrel of the rifle and hearing the hammer snap down. Every time he thought of that moment his heart stopped for a fraction of a second and he felt sick with fear. His uncle was the only one who seemed to understand — almost the only one. The half-breed boy knew and understood. He had faced the same helpless death from Snell's bayonet.

Tom cleared these thoughts from his head as he approached the Captain's tent. To his surprise, the enemy prisoner stood outside the tent. He wore large cast off boots and an old tattered army jacket. The Captain emerged from the tent as soon as Tom arrived.

"Ah, young Kerslake — just in time — where's your bugle?"

"Sorry Sir, I didn't know you needed me to play. I was just told to report to your tent."

"Blast it!" Lashbrooke turned toward the prisoner. "And you! You look like a tramp! I want him to look like a plains warrior! Get out of those work clothes and into something decent."

The officer commanding the Montreal Artillery came out of Lashbrooke's tent.

"What's the trouble?"

"They're not ready," snapped Lashbrooke. Tom was completely confused. Ready for what? What difference did it make about clothing for a prisoner?

"No matter," replied the artillery officer. "It'll take me a few minutes to get the camera set up. Plenty of time for them to change."

"Oh, alright, but let's hurry," said Lashbrooke nervously. He turned to Tom.

"This is Captain Peters, the famous photographer. He's going to shoot a picture of the first prisoner of war taken in the campaign. He also wants you in the photograph since you were involved and — ah me too as the *on site* commander of course."

"I see the Sergeant Major and Corporal Snell aren't here yet. Shall I fetch them, Sir?"

The Captain, suddenly busy brushing lint from his tunic, ignored the question. A suspicion formed in Tom's mind. Did his uncle or Snell know about the picture?

"Excuse me, Sir. Did you want me to find the Sergeant Major and . . . ."

"No, I do not. Your uncle is unfortunately gone on other duties this afternoon, and I refuse to have that blackguard Snell involved at all."

The Captain would not meet Tom's eye. His face flushed and he tweeked his moustaches furiously. Tom stood his ground.

"We have to take the photograph now — the light is perfect." He waved vaguely at the sun. "Also, Captain Peters is very busy and. . ." his voice trailed off lamely. Tom kept his mouth shut and stared hard at the squirming officer. The old silent treatment. It worked even better on Lashbrooke than it did on Vi.

"Bah! I don't have to explain my actions to you. Now, I want you to take the prisoner and find his good clothes. Make sure he wears that red sash thing and lend him a hat. Then get back here with your bugle."

Tom did as he was told, and Captain Peters took two pictures. In one, the prisoner simply stood between the Captain and Tom. In the second, Luc was kneeling while Tom stood beside him holding his bugle up as though to blow it. Captain Lashbrooke stood behind them brandishing his sword very dramatically. As soon as the pictures were taken, Lashbrooke was in a panic to send everyone away.

The pictures were to be published back east. The Captain was afraid that if the General knew of the photographs, he would stop publication. The General had already forbidden Lashbrooke from talking to a Winnipeg newspaper reporter who had arrived at the camp a few days ago.

"Go on now — off with you Kerslake!" Tom was watching Captain Peters advance the photograph tray on his camera.

"And where is the prisoner's guard? Guard!" Lashbrooke bellowed angrily. "Prisoner's Guard! Report to me!"

Several soldiers were standing nearby, but the guard was nowhere to be seen.

"Well, I can't wait all day for him." He turned to the prisoner. "Where did your guard go?"

Luc shrugged. "I don't know Monsieur. He watches me, I don't watch. . . ."

"Oh blast it! Here comes the General!" Lashbrooke grabbed Luc's arm. "Listen, do you know Captain Fraser?"

"Oui, Monsieur."

"Right then, report directly to him. He's Duty Officer in that tent there." He pointed to a square tent a short distance away.

"Hurry now, on the double. I'm watching you."

The prisoner jogged past Tom. Captain Peters was tipping a new photographic plate into the exposure chamber. What an amazing gadget this camera was, so small and easy to operate. Father loved mechanical things, maybe they could buy one.

"Bugler Kerslake!" Lashbrooke shouted. "I told you to clear this area. Now do so, immediately!"

Tom saluted and turned away smartly. He walked back down G Company's tent line and carefully stowed his bugle in his bedroll. He had a half hour before drill so he strolled to the river bank. The camp was perched

on a plateau high above the river and from the banks he
could see for miles across the wide valley.

A path descended the steep bluff to the water's edge
where a work party was building a log dock. Captain
Fraser was supervising them.

Captain Fraser!

Tom looked for the prisoner, but he wasn't there.
Legs churning like a windmill, he raced headlong down
the path.

"Captain Fraser!" The officer looked up.

"Have you seen the rebel prisoner?" Tom pounded
up to the dock. "He was supposed to report to you."

"Me? No, I've been here the last hour."

"He wandered off — during the photographs!" Tom
panted.

Fraser grasped Tom's shoulder. "Slow down, what
are you talking about? Where's the guard?"

"Captain Lashbrooke told the prisoner to see you,
at the duty officer tent because he couldn't find the guard,
but. . . ."

"Thunderation!" Fraser kicked at a log. "You men,
come with me. Surely he can't just walk out of an army
camp in broad daylight."

* * *

Luc pulled his borrowed hat low over his eyes and
trotted past Tom, who was peering over the photographer's
shoulder at the camera. He kept running — past the Duty

Officer's tent and turned off the camp main street. Now
he walked, not too fast yet not too slow.

His nerves were as taut as a fiddle string. Every step
he took, he expected to be discovered, but no soldier even
glanced his way. Many civilians stayed in the camp and
Luc looked like any one of them. So far he had been
lucky and his luck held, for Marie was alone at the
Larouche tent, cutting firewood. He darted up behind
her silently as she swung the big axe.

"Marie, it's me!" he hissed. "We must run, now!"

Marie gasped in surprise, dropping the axe.

"Luc. Are you crazy? How did you get here?"

Luc's stomach was twisted in a knot of fear. He
wanted to scream; they had no time for questions. He
felt the urge just to take her hand and run away, but that
wouldn't work. Forcing down his panic, he spoke quickly
but clearly.

"I'll hide in your tent. You gather some food, hurry
now, and give it to me. Then go get your father's horse
and bring it here. We can ride out together past the south
end of the soldiers' horse picket. There's no guard there,
I've watched it for a week now."

Marie was bewildered. "This is crazy! They'll catch
us or shoot us! I can't just leave my mother to run off
with you, not right now."

Luc felt the panic rising again, but he had to stay
calm and convince Marie to come with him, he couldn't
go without her. "Why not? I don't understand? Your

father has betrayed us. He's joined with the English. You said you would escape with me, what's wrong?"

Marie hesitated, as though she was afraid to answer him. "Maman needs my help, and they need the money I earn working for the priests."

"But you can't work for the priests if you're stuck here!" Luc snapped in exasperation. "Come with me back to Batoche. You can stay with the priests until the war is over. Then maybe your mother will come home. And my parents will take care of you. You can't stay with the enemy."

"No! It's more than that. I have to take care of her, protect her!"

Luc was baffled. "Protect her? From who, the soldiers? They won't hurt her."

"Not the soldiers. From my father!" She shouted in anger and frustration. Luc was stunned. He didn't understand but he could see the hurt and fear in Marie's eyes.

"I protect her from my father, Luc," she said in a tiny voice that quivered on the edge of crying. Luc could see the tears welling up in her eyes. Her fists were clenched so hard that her knuckles turned white and she bit her lip to hold the tears back.

They stood silently facing each other. Luc's mind was a swirl of confusion. The soldiers might come at any moment, Marie was caught in some horrible trap between her mother and her brutish father, and he couldn't leave without her. Suddenly Marie's eyes opened wide in surprise and she rapidly blinked the tears away.

"Oh no! It's him, it's my father. He's coming this way and it looks like he's been drinking. Don't turn around or he'll see you. Quick hide in our tent, I'll get rid of him."

Luc darted into the Larouche tent and hid himself in the corner.

"Marie!" It was Larouche's harsh, gravel voice. "Where's my horse? Get him saddled and ready to go! I've got to ride out on a mission with the Scouts. That idiot Goyette is trying to escape — but we'll catch him."

"I won't help you hunt down one of our own people!" Luc could hear the defiance in Marie's voice. "Saddle your own horse."

"You lazy brat!" Larouche cursed her. "When I give you a job I want it done!"

Luc heard a smack. Marie fell heavily to the ground just outside the open tent flap. A thin stream of blood trickled from her lip. Luc was sickened. He suddenly understood why Marie thought she had to protect her mother. Before Marie could get to her feet, Luc dashed out of the tent.

He took Larouche by surprise. Luc smashed head-first into the big man's belly. They went down together with a crash; Luc flinging punches wildly.

"Goyette!" The cry was a mixture of surprise and triumph. Larouche locked one powerful arm around Luc's neck and in a moment pinned him to the ground.

"Guards! Soldiers! I've captured your escaped prisoner!" The voice roared loudly. "Michel Larouche has saved the day, come quickly!" He cackled and spoke cheerfully to Luc. "You've made me a hero. They'll pay me a big reward. You're an escaping spy and they'll hang you for sure, Goyette."

Luc struggled but it was hopeless. Larouche was as strong as a bear.

"Oh Luc — how foolish." He looked up over Larouche's grubby arm to see Marie standing above them. She wasn't crying, but the sadness in her eyes cut to his heart. She turned slowly away as a crowd of soldiers ran toward them. She pulled a rosary from her pocket and he heard her faint voice. "Hail Mary full of grace, the Lord is with thee, . . .

She was praying for him, foolish, doomed sinner that he was.

* * *

There was no talk of hanging but they took Luc's knife and doubled his guard, day and night. No visitors, no Marie, and more work. There was a jail in Saskatoon and he was to be sent there. The English camp was bad enough, he'd suffocate locked up in a cell! He'd have to make a better plan for escape, and figure a way to see Marie.

As it turned out, it was Marie who found ways to visit him over the next few days, and it was she who planned their escape. Each morning and afternoon she would walk out to where Luc was working. The soldiers were always happy to see her, and not only because she was pretty. She also usually brought the guard a fresh biscuit, or a piece of real bread, anything that would tempt them into letting her talk to Luc for a few minutes.

They spoke in French or Cree or a mixture of both. Her father had been furious to find out that Luc was not being hanged and even more furious to discover that she had been visiting him. But she learned from him that the General planned to ship the wounded back to Saskatoon soon, and Luc would go with them.

She made herself useful around the hospital where they were short-handed, helping tend to the wounded. She convinced one of the doctors to ask for her as a helper on the trip back to Saskatoon. Her father had been suspicious but when the doctor offered to pay Marie a wage, and offered to pay that wage in advance to him, he had agreed quickly.

She had even managed to pack up a provision of food and hide it in the hospital stores. She thought it would be easier to escape from a hospital wagon train than from the armed camp. Luc's admiration for Marie's courage and good sense grew each day. His fate was in her hands now.

Their last day in the camp, Luc was put to work helping prepare the hospital wagons. He was stuffing makeshift mattresses with grass and straw.

"Well, well, look who's coming!" One of the guards nudged him. He straightened up from his work and saw Larouche approaching. The guard, a young soldier not much older than Luc, marched out to meet Marie's father. The other guard stayed with Luc.

"Hey, Michel le two faces! How much did the General reward you for capturing your own man?"

The soldier stopped Larouche and confronted him.

"I heard he paid you exactly what you're worth."

"Yeah — bugger all!" The guard near Luc called out the punch line and both soldiers laughed. Larouche ignored the laughter.

"Je veux dire . . . I want . . . talk." His face flushed red with anger and he pointed at Luc.

"Maybe he doesn't want to talk to you." The guard held his rifle up at the high port. "That's a real rebel there. He's a fighter, like us — he calls us the Little Black Devils."

"Yeah, clear off Larouche!" The guard nearest Luc hollered. "Send your daughter. We'll talk to Mam'zell Marie — but not to you."

"No! Please. I'll see him," Luc cut in quickly to stop them mocking.

"Pourquoi!" he demanded angrily when Larouche reached him. "Why do you let the Englishmen make fun of you?"

"Who cares about privates," Larouche waved at the soldiers. "I am an important scout. The General and the officers know that. They gave me a horse and good food for my family, better than being a slave like you."

"They despise you," Luc snapped. Could Larouche really think the English respected him? "And your own people will hate you."

"*Mahti Pahakitoon!*" He shoved Luc roughly. "They hate Larouche anyway. Dumont leaves the battle and he's a hero! But Michel Larouche leaves and he's a coward? No matter what I do, it's wrong, so I must look out for myself."

The young guard jumped between them, his rifle butt raised.

"What about Marie? Who looks out for her?"

"Stay away from her!" Larouche tried to push past the soldier. The second guard stepped in and thumped him in the ribs with the flat of his rifle stock.

"Enough! Get out of here!"

Larouche backed off, rubbing his side. "I came to warn you Goyette. Stay away from Marie!"

The young guard gave him a shove and he left muttering.

They were up before dawn the next day, loading the wounded. Marie was nowhere to be seen. What could

have happened to her? The wagons were soon lined up
and ready to go. A small escort of Boulton's men
accompanied them, but other than Luc's two guards,
there were no fighting soldiers with the train. The Scouts
led off and soon the guards were prodding Luc to move
along. His heart plunged. He was on his own again.

They had gone about a mile down the trail, when
two horses cantered up behind them. One was ridden
by the doctor who had hired Marie. Marie and her father
rode double on the second horse. The doctor was
furious. He leaped from his horse and stomped over to
one of the wagons, reappearing with a leather bag. He
took money from it, gave it to Larouche, and helped
Marie down from the horse. The doctor shouted some
angry words; but Larouche merely laughed and wheeled
his horse to ride back to the soldiers' camp.

Marie hurried past Luc to board one of the wagons.
She tried to turn away from him but he glimpsed her
face. One eye was blackened and swollen, and there was
a large bruise on her cheekbone. Luc felt sick. That was
Larouche's warning alright. But at least she was rid of
her father now. He swore that he would never let her go
back again.

They travelled without rest all day and stopped just
past Clark's Crossing when the sun started to set. The
teamsters circled the wagons and Boulton's men put out
sentries on the trail. Luc and his guards cut wood for the
hospital cooks' supper fire.

That evening when the camp had settled down, Marie came to see him. "Eh cherie — Bonjour." One of the guards whistled loudly, then flourished a deep bow. "When are you going to give up on this rebel? I'm the man for you!"

Marie blushed. She spoke almost no English — but she recognized a wolf when she saw one. The second guard shoved his partner aside.

"Forget both of 'em Mad-a-moi-cell." He took Marie's hand and bent to kiss it. She snatched it away and offered a cloth wrapped parcel in its place.

The soldier untied the cloth. "Fresh bread and molasses, Dick!"

Both guards sat happily on the ground devouring the food while she talked to Luc. He felt guilty when he saw her bruised face. Perhaps if he hadn't involved her in this, she wouldn't have been beaten.

"What did that animal do to you? I'll make him pay."

"Never mind that now," she replied calmly. "Speak Cree, these men might know some French. Now listen. Our best chance is tonight; the farther we get away from Batoche, the more difficult it will be to get back safely."

"What is your plan?"

"There are very few soldiers with the train. They're spread thinly and can't afford to leave the wagons unguarded. If we can escape they won't have enough men to search for us until they reach the base at Saskatoon. By then we'll be far away."

Luc smiled and nodded at the guards.

"Agreed, but what about my two friends? While one sleeps, the other is always awake."

"Simple. I'm not guarded. So after midnight, I'll slip out of camp and start a fire in the grass on the west side of the trail. I have a tin full of lantern oil. It'll make a good fire; the grass is dry, and the breeze is blowing up from the river valley."

She pointed to where the sunset disappeared beyond the far side of the camp. One of the guards looked up and she smiled nicely at him.

"Le pain — c'est bon ça? Is good?"

He held a thumb up and grinned. "Yeah, très good, darling."

Marie casually turned and gazed in the opposite direction.

"As soon as the sentries sound the alarm I'll come here and distract your guard for a few minutes. You must use that time to escape. Run to that large stand of poplars to the east of the camp and wait for me. I've already walked out to it and hidden our food there."

It was a great plan. It would work. He checked the position of the poplar woods, memorizing them. They might be difficult to find in the dark. They chatted for a few more minutes, then she left.

Luc rolled up in his blankets under the wagon that night and pretended sleep. The guard stood quietly by, smoking his pipe.

"Fire! Fire! Stand to! Stand to!"

The scout shouting the alarm was running along the wagons, rousing everyone. Luc sat up and banged his head on the wagon axle. He had fallen asleep! How could he have let himself fall asleep tonight? He scrambled from his blankets, rolled them up and tied them, ready for his escape. A line of brilliant yellow flames crept toward the camp from the direction of the river.

Scouts and teamsters were running around half dressed, some carrying rifles, others with sacking or shovels to put out the fire. It was a perfect confusion. Luc's guard was pacing back and forth, shouting questions to the others. Finally he knelt by the wagon and motioned for Luc to come out.

"Come on!" he yelled. "We're going to go help fight this fire before it reaches the camp. Hurry up!"

Luc crouched under the wagon. Why hadn't they foreseen this? If he left now, she'd never find him in all the confusion.

"Get out here now!" The guard reached under the wagon and grabbed Luc by the collar, pulling him clear.

Luc's mind was racing. "What about the Métis attackers?" he shouted.

The guard stopped short. "What are you talking about?"

"The Métis people start a prairie fire, then ambush the enemy when they try to run from it. Shouldn't you stay by the wagons to defend them?" He knew it was weak but it might buy some time. The soldier looked around nervously, as though the enemy might suddenly appear. The moment's delay was all they needed. Marie came running out of the dark.

She grabbed the soldier by the arm. "Kipa! Kichimokomana. L'hôpital pris feu! Weechihin pastawihaman li feu!"

The guard, of course, didn't understand a word and struggled to make out what she wanted. She kept pulling at his sleeve, dragging him away, and screaming at him as though she desperately needed his help.

It was Luc's chance. He ducked back under the wagon, grabbed his blanket and rolled out the other side. It was dark here, away from the flames. He couldn't see the woods but he sprinted off in the general direction.

Once he was clear of the wagons he stopped to let his eyes become accustomed to the night. He was free. Marie's plan was working. If only he could be sure *she* would get away. Gradually he was able to distinguish the skyline, and the rough black shape of the woods rising out of the prairie. He ran on till he reached the bushes, then knelt down, invisible in the dark, to watch for Marie.

The wagons were outlined against the yellow glow of the fire and he could hear the Englishmen yelling. Nobody seemed to be searching for him. After all, where would they start to look? He could be anywhere out on the dark prairie.

He didn't have to wait long. Someone approached off to his left. It had to be Marie, didn't it? The dark figure drew near. The memory of the Scouts at the Crossing came back. He shuddered. Footsteps crunched through the tall grass, then a faint whisper, "Luc, are you here?" She had come.

Dawn found them halfway back to Tourond's Coulee. They had circled well to the east of the main trail and would stay off the road until they neared Batoche. There had been no followers; in fact, now that he was free it was hard to imagine that he had been a prisoner. Nevertheless they took no chances and hid in another poplar bluff all day. They ate half of their food and slept. At sunset they moved off, knowing that by morning they would be safe at home, beyond the reach of the soldiers and Larouche.

They walked swiftly in the fading light. What would he find at home? His parents would take Marie in, that was certain. But would they be safe from the English army? Would Dumont fight? He smiled, of course Dumont would fight. More important, would Luc fight again?

No choice, really. It was the last chance for the Métis on the Saskatchewan. But even if they won, would life ever be the same again? He glanced at Marie. Whatever happened, his future now included her. That was certain.

* * *

"Hear the latest, little Kerslake?" Snell asked.

Tom, busy mending a tear in his tunic, looked up from his work. There had been so many rumours and stories circulating the last two weeks that he didn't believe anything he heard. "What now? I suppose we're all going to England to have tea with Queen Victoria?"

"Not likely! We'll probably stay here at Fish Creek for the rest of our lives." The Corporal sniffed and wiped his nose on his sleeve. "Naw, this is solid fact! Heard it from one of Boulton's men who escorted the wounded back to Saskatoon last week. About that little rebel we captured."

Tom stopped sewing. "Well, what is it?"

"Those idiots that were supposed to be guarding him, let him escape. Had a fire or something one night and he just sneaked off into the dark. They were afraid to leave the wagons to go look for him." Snell spat to show his contempt for the guards. Tom thought of the tattered boy who had fought so bravely, and smiled.

Snell noticed. "Oh I forgot, you were his bosom pal! This is good news for you, I suppose." His voice took a hard edge. "Well, here's some more news for you. If I get another chance with my bayonet at him or any other rebel don't get in my way. 'Cause he won't escape twice." Snell turned on his heel to leave, but Tom stopped him.

"Did they say if Patrick Flaherty made it to the hospital?"

"Ya, it was touch and go, but he was still alive. The doctors at Saskatoon said he had a fifty-fifty chance." Both Tom and the Corporal fell silent. Eventually Snell spat again, then left.

Tom pushed the thoughts of dying soldiers and future battles from his mind and went for a walk to the riverbank. Spring was finally coming. The trees in the river valley were threatening to sprout leaves. He had thought many times over the last two weeks how beautiful and fertile this river valley was and had even discussed homesteading with his uncle. After the fighting stopped, of course. And only if they won, and if his father would agree to move out of Winnipeg.

"Tom!" Uncle Jim's shout interrupted his daydream. "Pack up your gear tonight. We march on Batoche tomorrow morning."

Epilogue Fact and Fiction

The 90th Battalion Winnipeg Rifles marched off to war just as the story tells, but with six companies, (A to F). G Company, Captain Lashbrooke and the Kerslakes never existed. The soldiers were so eager that most of the regiments actually had men "stowaway" on the train rather than be left behind, as Tom did. The map of the battlefield at Fish Creek is a copy of maps actually drawn by one of General Middleton's officers, Captain Haig, in 1885.

Of the army troops engaged at Fish Creek every seventh man was killed or wounded. Although it was a small battle, it was fierce. The fighting was much as it is described in this book. And there really were young bugler boys from the 90th Winnipeg Rifles who fought at Fish Creek. One, named Billy Buchanan, showed such courage under fire that General Middleton commended him in his official report of the battle. To be "Mentioned in Dispatches" is considered to be an important distinction.

The 90th Battalion Winnipeg Rifles exists today as the Royal Winnipeg Rifles. They are still a militia infantry battalion and they have fought in many of Canada's battles since Fish Creek, but Fish Creek was their first. Their badge has the emblem of a Black Devil on it. Their motto is "Named by the enemy in Battle."

* * *

The Métis people of the Saskatchewan River valley took up arms in 1885 just as this story says though Luc, Pierre and the Larouches never really existed. Métis men did scout the army at Clark's Crossing and the map of the Crossing is a copy of the actual map found in Louis Riel's papers after the war. It was drawn by one of the teamsters who was a spy. Nobody knows how he smuggled it out of the army camp to Riel.

There was a Dakota warrior who was killed at Fish Creek exactly as Luc saw it happen, and it's true that just forty-five men fought the whole day against terrific odds without giving up. And there were young warriors on the Métis side. One of the Tourond brothers tells of a Sioux boy only twelve years old who was at Fish Creek! Also, the Boyer mentioned in the story as being killed at Fish Creek was actually Joseph Boyer. He was a very young man when he died from his wounds. He lies buried in Batoche. His name, and those of the other Métis soldiers killed at Fish Creek, are carved on a memorial stone in the graveyard there.

The Métis army fought again at Batoche in a four day battle. That battle shattered their army and they suffered many casualties. Riel and Dumont escaped. Riel gave himself up and was hanged for treason. Dumont lived in the United States and even worked for Buffalo Bill Cody's Wild West Show before he returned to Batoche. The controversy over Métis and Indian land rights still continues today.

* * *

The battlefield today is very much like it was in 1885. The places where Luc and Pierre made their shelter; where Tom and G Company charged; and where the artillery worked their guns are easy to see. Not far from the battlefield, near the river, a monument marks the place the army camped after the battle. It carries the names of Canadian Army soldiers killed at Fish Creek.

Glossary

Api	Sit, Cree
Bichon	Light or tan colour of horses, Métis
Capote	Cloak, French
Ceinture noue	Sash, French
Awas	Expression of contempt, Cree
Uneeyen	Riel, Cree
Waniska	Get up, Cree
N'Sjayasis	Little Brother, Cree
Ekaya	Stop, Cree
Mistahyamaskwa	Big Bear, Cree
Galette	Wheatcake, French
Nisitoothten	I understand, Cree
Ekwana	Leave him alone, Cree
Atim	Dog, (insult), Cree
Poltrons	Cowards, French
Faon	Fawn, French
Neeak	Go, Cree
Cochon	Pig, French
Petit Oie	Silly boy (lit. "little goose"), French
Éclaireurs	Scouts, French
Jeune Chasseur	Young soldier
Niskapesim	Goose Moon, (April), Cree
Owasis	Youngster, Cree
Soketahawin	Courage, Cree
Kipa	Hurry, Cree
Vendu	Traitor, (lit. "Sell out"), French

En Apola	A method of roasting pieces of meat on the end of a stick over a fire, French words – Métis phrase
Sioux	The word means "Snake" which was a mild insult. Their real name was Dakota.
Maskiki	Strong medicine, Cree
Zareba	Temporary fort made of wagons and palisades. Originally an African word, used by the British Army.
Mahti Pahakitoon	Shut up! Cree
Kichimokomana	Soldier, Cree
L'hôpital pris feu	The hospital is on fire, French
Weechihin	Help me, Cree
Pastawihaman	Put out, Cree

"Courage Chasseurs! Ne craignez pas le tapage;
Du Canon de ces Anglais."– Be Brave Soldiers! Do
not fear the roar; of the English Cannons.

This is part of an old French song from the
Napoleonic wars which the Métis sang at the battle of
Fish Creek to help their morale.